SUBMITTING TO THE LAWYER

Cowboy Doms, Book Four

BJ WANE

Published by Blushing Books
An Imprint of
ABCD Graphics and Design, Inc.
A Virginia Corporation
977 Seminole Trail #233
Charlottesville, VA 22901

BJ Wane
Submitting to the Lawyer

EBook ISBN: 978-1-64563-046-3
Print ISBN: 978-1-64563-074-6
v1

Dan Shylock entered the playroom of his BDSM club tired and unsure why he'd bothered to come out tonight. He'd had his hands full with trying two court cases this week and continuing his newest employees' education in small ranching. If it weren't for Bernie, his reliable, trustworthy foreman of the past nine years, he wouldn't be able to juggle both a legal career and a working ranch. After noting the crowd spread out in the converted barn, he veered toward a quiet, secluded corner, taking a seat on a sofa that faced the room. Leaning back with a sigh, he crossed one booted ankle over his opposite knee and stretched his arms out behind him. Scanning the Saturday night members, he spotted his friends, the Dunbar brothers at the circular bar in the center of the floor, their wives at their sides, like usual. It tickled him how content the two confirmed bachelors now were with wedded bliss. He could see why they had succumbed so fast to the charms of Sydney and Tamara, just not why they'd been in such a hurry to make that commitment. Although, he mused, Connor's downfall hadn't come nearly as quick or as easy as Caden's. You'd think, maintaining such a close friendship with the neighbor girl for years would have made the decision to take their relationship to the next level a no-brainer, but the younger Dunbar had fought against going that route and it almost cost him their special connection for good.

The image of a golden-eyed brunette popped into his head, a common occurrence lately. He'd thought he and Nan Meyers also enjoyed a close bond, both as frequent Dom/sub partners here at The Barn and as friends outside of the sexually charged atmosphere. But the longer she stayed away and out of touch, the more he questioned what was going on with her and why she had shut him out along with her other friends. She'd left Willow Springs last summer, right after the Dunbar's double wedding, to spend a few weeks with her brother in New Orleans and hadn't returned in the ten months since. Every time he went by her closed up tea shop located not far from his office in the town square, his gut tightened as he thought of her abrupt silence following the first few weeks of her departure.

"You'll scare the subs away with that scowl," Sheriff Grayson Monroe drawled as he took a seat next to Dan.

"Nah, they love all of us just the way we are." Dan flicked him a sideways glance. "Where's your pretty wife? Never mind, I see her now."

With her soft, round curves displayed nicely in a red teddy, Avery padded up to them carrying a soft drink and beer, handing the beer to Grayson with a blush as Dan enjoyed a slow look at her delectable body. "Evening, Avery."

"Hi, Master Dan." Grayson tugged her onto his lap and wrapped an arm around her waist. "How are you?" she asked, leaning against her husband with a contented sigh.

"I'd be better if you were still single, or if Master Grayson would share once in a while," he teased just to watch her face turn a deeper shade of red. "I swear, this place used to be more fun before everyone decided to settle down with their subs." The sheriff hadn't waited long after the Dunbars to put a ring on Avery's finger and the couple had married last fall.

"Maybe you'd enjoy yourself more if you would start playing again. When was the last time you made one of our subs happy?" Grayson never did believe in beating around the bush.

Dan frowned, thinking back. Had it been that long since he'd indulged himself here? There had been a few nights when he hadn't been in the mood for anything except socializing, and with his caseload, he hadn't frequented the club as much in the last two months. Between the physical exertion of ranching and keeping up with his law practice, he stayed busy.

Shrugging, he lowered his arms and leg to lean forward, bracing his forearms on his thighs. "I guess it has been a few weeks," he admitted with a rueful shake of his head.

Grayson reached up and cupped Avery's breast through the silky material, rasping his thumb over her nipple until the pouty bud hardened. "You kept to yourself a lot right after Nan left as well. Everyone misses her. Still no word?"

Well, yeah, he missed her too. She was the only sub he didn't shy away from playing with on a regular basis, mainly because she shared his enjoyment of remaining free of entanglements. The delightful way she embraced her submissiveness and her penchant for pain play and rough sex made her the perfect match for his strict dominance.

"I haven't heard from her, and last I checked with Tamara, neither had she," he replied, his irritation with Nan's silence underscoring his words. "I'm just tired tonight. It's been a long, stressful week."

"How are the military parolees working for you? Getting the hang of things?" Sliding his hand downward, Grayson idly caressed the inside of Avery's thigh, the slow circular motions drawing Dan's gaze.

Shifting, he felt the first stirrings of interest in choosing someone to scene with. "Yeah. Their time in an Army jail for possession followed by a stint in rehab took its toll, just like the others I've hired following their release. Morales is doing well but Pete has lapsed twice. I'm holding out hope he'll come around, though. They deserve a second chance for cleaning up their act, or, at least trying to." Dan and Grayson both spent years in the military. During his time as a JAG officer, he'd both defended and prosecuted numerous military recruits on drug charges while Grayson had seen combat firsthand. It hadn't taken him long to understand how the atrocities of war could drive even the most stalwart of young people into substance abuse in order to cope.

"I get it, they still need supervision. I admire your commitment, but don't envy you the job." With a nudge, Grayson prodded Avery up and stood to clasp her hand. "Caden has you down to monitor the loft in about fifteen minutes. Does that work?"

Dan nodded. "Sure, I'll be up. Catch you later." He winked at Avery and watched his friends head for the stairs leading to the upper level of the converted barn.

The Dunbar brothers and Grayson were already in the middle of renovating the dilapidated barn when he purchased his property, but as soon as he'd gotten wind of the project, he didn't hesitate to offer his help. The members took turns keeping an eye on scenes, especially those using the bondage equipment. They were a close-knit group and everyone knew and adhered to the rules of the club and the well-known guidelines that ensured safe BDSM play, but that didn't mean mistakes weren't made or something consensual couldn't get out of hand.

Pushing to his feet, Dan decided he'd stayed to himself long enough and strolled toward the bar, noticing Caden leading Sydney out back. He knew the pretty redhead enjoyed the hot tub, and it appeared her husband was in the mood to indulge her. An excellent chef, she likely bribed him with a favorite dish or dessert. If he employed as many hands as the Dunbars, he would hire her in a heartbeat to cook for them. His small cattle herd was manageable with five cowpunchers, just large enough to enable him to indulge in both his love of ranching and practicing law.

Sliding onto a barstool next to Tamara, he tugged on her black braid and flashed her a quick grin. "Why don't you dump your Dom and play with me tonight? Aren't you tired of him yet?" He tilted his head toward Connor behind the bar.

She returned his smile, her gray eyes lit with pleasure as she gazed at her husband. "He is tiresome," she replied with a mock sigh. "But I waited too long to get him into bed to give him up now that I have him there. But, thanks anyway."

"Did I mention the new spanker I picked up this week, sweetie?" Connor whipped his blue eyes from Tamara to Dan. "Master Dan, why don't you find your own girl to pester? I think I heard Leslie mention your name earlier."

"Get me a beer and I may indulge her after I monitor." Dan clasped the cold bottle Connor handed over and took a swig before saluting the couple with the brew. "Thanks."

Winding his way toward the stairs, Dan took in the gyrating couples dancing to a pulse-pounding beat, trying to remember the last time he enjoyed a sub sliding her soft body against his to the tune of a sultry voice. He had a fondness for slow dancing, but it had been ages since he'd indulged in that pleasure. Frowning, he took the stairs up to the loft, trying to remember when the last time was. *Surely it wasn't with Nan.* Had it really been all those months ago, before she'd taken off? Taking another long pull on his beer, he wondered at himself, and vowed if she ever got her enticing ass back here, she would answer for occupying his mind way too much with worry for her. As far as he knew, she hadn't been in touch with any of her closest friends for some time now either, which wasn't like her.

Greg Young, a newer member of the club, met him in the center of the dim loft, both of them eying Master Brett for a moment as he wielded a slim cane across his wife, Sue Ellen's round buttocks. Bound facing the wall, she embraced each swat with a soft cry and lift of her ass for more. A year ago, the middle-aged couple was the only pair in a committed relationship.

"Are you here to relieve me?" Greg asked, tilting his auburn head with a grin tugging at his lips as Brett released his wife and she cuddled against him with a glazed expression.

"I am." Clapping him on the shoulder, Dan said, "Go on. I imagine you and Devin are ready to send someone into subspace." The two close friends often shared a woman between them, and from what Dan had witnessed, their subs always went away content and happy.

"We do aim to please. It's been quiet up here." A high-pitched cry of release resonated from the far corner where the webbed fucking swing was being put to good use. "Well," Greg drawled, "relatively quiet, anyway. Later."

Dan waved him off and settled against the back wall. Tipping his Stetson down, he crossed his arms and scanned the activities with slow perusal, noting who was where and what scenes they were playing out. He enjoyed this time of observance, watching others play, maybe choosing his own next partner and a scene from what he witnessed. But as the hour wound down, he was contemplating calling it a night instead, unable to set aside his exhaustion from the busy week and the mental dissatisfaction plaguing him tonight.

Caden appeared upstairs, ready to take over just as Leslie approached Dan with a lustful interest reflected in her blue eyes any self-respecting Dom would find difficult to ignore.

"Master Dan, how are you?"

Her voice was as soft as her lush body and Dan held out his hand to her without thinking about it. "I'm good, Leslie. Care to join me?"

Her eyes lit with excitement as she clasped his hand. "I'd like that, Sir."

He looked toward Caden and received his affirmative nod before tugging Leslie over to a chain station, intending to put the flogger swishing against his side to good use and an end to his odd mood. He knew from topping her before how much Leslie relished the snap of leather against her bare skin. Almost as much as Nan, making him wonder if his long absent, favorite sub had been getting her needs met these many months away. Disgusted with himself for thinking about another when his focus should be on the girl who had entrusted herself to his care now, he whisked Leslie's breast hugging, spandex top over her head, freeing the plump mounds with an enticing bounce.

"Just as pretty as I remember." Cupping both breasts, he kept his eyes on her face as he kneaded her malleable flesh before plucking the sensitive tips into hardened buds. "More?" he asked, preferring his partners to vocalize their needs.

She leaned into him with a moan, her eyes glazing over. "Yes, please, Sir."

Dan twisted her nipples until she flinched and then held the tight pinch for three seconds. "Good girl," he praised her when she remained still and quiet. He suppressed a satisfied grin as he released the pale pink buds and she exhaled with a relieved breath. "Arms up and I'll give you what you need."

Her eyes flicked down to his flogger and a delicate shudder went through her. Raising her arms, she allowed him to bind her wrists, her breathing speeding up with anticipation as he skimmed his hands down her swaying torso to loosen her shorts. Shoving them down along with her thong, he reached behind her and curved his palms over her buttocks, squeezing hard enough to make her yelp. He loved those startled cries he could pull from a sub, especially when she embraced whatever he was doing to cause them.

Shifting his hands to Leslie's hips, Dan spun her around to face the wall. Leaning against her back, he bent his head to nip the tender skin between shoulder and neck and felt her shiver.

Satisfied with the response, he stepped back, unhooking the flogger from his waist.

"Soft and slow or hard and fast?" He gave her the choice as he trailed the braided strands over her buttocks and watched the soft mounds clench.

"Um… maybe a little of both?"

It always seemed to fluster some subs when he let them choose before starting instead of working them into accepting more as he went along. He didn't do it often, but he found himself reluctant to draw this scene out. A nagging sense of disquiet kept intruding to disrupt his thoughts, and it wouldn't be right to put her through her paces if his own head wasn't fully in the game.

With a flick of his wrist, he snapped the flogger across both cheeks hard enough to leave red stripes, soft enough to draw a moan of pleasure instead of a low groan of discomfort. "Yes, I now recall that about you. More heat, less sting. Got it."

Dan worked the flogger over her ass and thighs, inching up to her lower back for lighter strokes. Leslie swayed in the restraints, her hips jutting back to accept the lashes and then jerking forward as she gasped and allowed the prickling warmth to seep into her muscles. He preferred raising a deeper hue than the faint blush encompassing her backside, but then, these scenes weren't about him, at least not at this stage. By the time he finished delivering twelve strokes, a light sheen of perspiration coated her back and slick cream glistened at the seam of her puffy labia.

Dan returned the flogger to the hook at his waist and brushed his fingers over her quivering flesh, enjoying the warmth and Leslie's shudder before sliding his middle finger down her crack. With a twist of his hand, he slid a finger between her damp folds and pushed past her puckered anus' tight resistance with his thumb and set up a series of short jabs meant to tease and torment.

"Oh, God, please, Sir," Leslie gasped, thrusting back against his marauding hand.

"Please, what?" he demanded, clutching her hip with his free hand to hold her still. "More of this?" He withdrew from both orifices and then rammed back inside harder, deeper, bringing her to her toes with a cry.

"Yes, yes, please…"

One of his favorite perks of being a Dom was playing with a sub for long periods of time, tormenting them by dragging out their release, or withholding it at his whim or in accordance with their needs or actions. Leslie was a sweet girl, always eager to play and please, but instead of taking his time to enjoy her, he zeroed in on her clit, giving in to her pleas with little thought, just a sudden desire to move this along.

Annoyed with himself, he demanded in a tone harsher than intended, "Come for me, Leslie." He rubbed her clit harder, faster, until she gushed over his finger and her strained cry resonated around them.

Dan stroked inside Leslie's clasping pussy as she settled down from her climax, playing with her silky sheath until the small ripples ceased and she shuddered with a sigh of sated contentment. As soon as she calmed and turned to him with a grateful smile, he released her arms and held her shaking body close. Despite his semi-erection, he didn't feel a pressing need to indulge in his own pleasure. Instead, exhaustion crept back in, prodding him to make it an early night.

Tilting her face up, he kissed her cheek, noticing her clear eyes. "Let me help you dress, hon."

"Sir, I'd be happy to reciprocate," Leslie offered, inching her hand down his waist.

He grabbed her wrist but smiled to soften his refusal. "I know, and appreciate it, but I'm good." At least, that's what he kept telling himself.

Nothing has changed. Nan Meyers breathed a sigh of relief as she peered out the taxi window as they drove through her small hometown of Willow Springs, Montana on a quiet Monday morning. There had been so many changes in her life the ten months she'd been away, she didn't think she could handle it if she'd finally gotten the nerve to return home and found a lot of things weren't as she'd left them. She needed the soothing comfort of small-town living, the embrace of warm friendships and the time to find herself again more than a spring blossom needed the sun to survive.

Looping around the quaint town square with its gurgling fountain and century-old buildings, she instructed the cab driver to take her around the back of the block of small shops and businesses. Parking behind the tea shop she inherited from her grandmother, she grabbed her bag and got out, handing him his fare through the window.

"Thank you. Have a nice day."

She waited in the empty alley until he drove away, standing next to her car where she'd left it parked so long ago. She'd timed her arrival during mid-morning, when everyone would be at work and few people were out and about shopping yet. With her emotions in a turmoil and her confidence still shattered into a million pieces, she needed to get her bearings before seeing anyone she knew well yet.

Nan took a moment to bask in the mid-May sun warming her face before clutching her suitcase and reaching for her keys. When she'd left for a short visit with her brother in New Orleans last summer, she had only planned on being away for a few weeks, thus the one bag. Getting involved with Gerard Avet and her own stupidity kept her away much longer. A shudder ran through her as the memories she was determined to overcome flitted through her head. Her brother, Jay had begged her to hold off a little longer on returning, insisting she wasn't ready to go it alone. But she wanted her life back, and her life was here, in the beloved town where they'd both grown up before Jay left for college and their parents died in a car accident a few short months after retiring.

Nan inserted the key and let herself into the back door of the two-story shop, veering left and up the rear stairs to the apartment she'd lived in with her grandmother following the loss of her parents shortly after her seventeenth birthday. With Jay settling in New Orleans following college instead of coming back home to Montana, it had been just the two of them the last seven years of Nana's life. Jay visited often and the three of them had remained close, sharing the burden of grief along with the cherished memories of their family, but Nana passed away over eight years ago and Nan returned to the apartment with a stab of nostalgia.

Opening the door, she was unprepared to face the darkened interior, the flash of instant terror keeping her rooted on the threshold. Gripping the doorknob, she sucked in a deep breath, fighting off the throat clogging fear threatening to choke her. *I'm fine, this is home. Gerard is in New Orleans awaiting trial.* The silent assurances did little to calm her racing heart or settle the nausea churning in her stomach that darkness always produced. She had spent three long, terror and pain-ridden days locked in Gerard's pitch-black basement before her rescue, long enough for fear to become entrenched into her soul with a tight clutch she'd failed to loosen in all the months since.

Sliding a shaky hand along the inside wall, she found the light switch by touch and flicked it on. The center bulb in the overhead fan lit up, dispelling the dark and easing her terror as she scanned the combined living, dining and kitchen room and breathed in the musty odor of a closed-up space. There was no distant sound of slow dripping water or the dank smell of an unfinished cellar. Shaking off the paralyzing remnants of her neurosis, she entered the small cozy home, set her suitcase down and went straight to the window to shove the blinds up and let in some much-needed fresh air and sunshine. The last of her jittery nerves settled down with the incoming breeze and bright swath of light spreading across the hardwood floor.

"Much better," she said aloud with a decisive nod, gazing out at the mountains towering behind the buildings of the square below.

New Orleans might be rich with history and offer an array of twenty-four-seven entertainment, but Nan still preferred the wide-open, less populated spaces she'd known her whole life. For fun, there were large barbeques at the neighboring ranches and riding pell-mell across a prairie dotted with daisies and glimpsing elk among the Ponderosa Pines or Douglas Firs. The annual county fair brought a crowd from the nearest towns in the spring and with both the Red Lodge Mountain and the newest dude ranch within a thirty-minute drive, they enjoyed tourism benefits year-round.

Thinking of the new ranch and lodge that opened right before she left reminded her of meeting the owners, Greg Young and Devin Fisher, and the one ménage she'd indulged in when they'd become members of The Barn. Just thinking about the kink club owned by her closest friends' now husbands drew a ripple of longing through her. Leaning her forehead on the windowpane, Nan closed her eyes and recalled the fun and plea-sures she had indulged in as a member of the nearest BDSM club. Master Clayton, who moved away a year after the club opened, had tutored her into accepting and then embracing her sexual submissive needs, and taught her not to be ashamed of getting those needs met through pain, bondage and dominance.

It had taken Master Gerard just one short week to strip her of everything she craved and cherished about the lifestyle she'd reveled in for five years.

Pivoting from the window, Nan turned her mind to the tasks of settling back into her apartment before venturing downstairs and getting to work on what needed to be done to open her tea shop again. Her phone rang as she started to toss her purse on the kitchen counter. Pulling it out, she wasn't at all surprised to see Jay's name pop up. "Hello, big brother," she answered with a warm smile.

"You got in okay? How are you holding up?" he asked, getting right to the point.

Discounting that brief lapse into fear at the door, she answered him with all honesty. "Yes, my flight arrived in Billings with no problem and I just got home. Other than looking around at the cleaning I need to do, I'm fine. But I love you for caring."

"Always, sis. I'm a plane ride away if you need me. Don't hesitate to call if you can't cope."

Nan stiffened against his good intentions. Damn it, she vowed. She *would* get her act together, and her life back, one way or another, without continuing to lean on her brother. "I have to do this, Jay. You know that."

His sigh came through the line. "Yeah, I know. That doesn't make it any easier. Remember, I saw the state you were in when we got you out of Avet's house."

She didn't need the reminder. She would carry the scars on her back forever, mementos of the mistake she'd made in trusting the wrong person. "Trust me, I remember. I'll call after I get settled back in, I promise."

"I'll hold you to it. Bye, sis."

Nan hung up feeling better just from hearing her big brother's voice. She would give anything if Jay moved back to Willow Springs but had given up trying to persuade him. He'd tried just as hard to entice her into relocating to New Orleans, but just as he'd made a life for himself there, she fostered no desire to start over anywhere else.

Brushing her hands down her jean-clad thighs, she tightened her jaw with determination and muttered aloud, "Okay, down to work."

Chapter 2

Nan spent all of Monday doing nothing but cleaning, both her apartment and the tea shop. The good news was she fell into an exhausted sleep without nightmares and woke refreshed this morning, eager to get her butt in gear. She brought back a variety of new teas, a sampling of gourmet coffees and a large assortment of French cookies to sell in the shop, but after taking inventory yesterday and throwing away almost everything still shelved, she spent the morning in Billings on a shopping trip.

As she carried in her purchases, she knew she should let her friends know she was back, but every time she thought of calling, she cringed. They'd texted and spoken often the first few weeks she'd been in New Orleans, but after her ordeal with Gerard, she hadn't had it in her to talk to anyone from home. Her silence these past months would be hard to explain without revealing too much.

She didn't worry as much about her three closest friends insisting on answers – they wouldn't be happy with her but would accept her need to come forth with the whole story in her own time. Master Dan might not be so understanding. It shouldn't have surprised her to find herself missing him the most, thinking about him the most during those traumatizing days and subsequent recovery. One reason she had searched out a BDSM group was because she'd needed a diversion from thinking about him so much.

Of the Doms Nan had submitted to at The Barn, he was not only her favorite, but knew her needs, and how to meet them the best. Despite the number of years she'd known the owners, both Dunbar brothers and Sheriff Monroe, Dan was the only one whose friendship outside of the club went a step beyond casual and stayed a comfortable margin short of committed. They'd met after her initial training and over the years had enjoyed each other enough to keep them interested in coming back for more.

Nan knew he wouldn't accept an evasive explanation for her actions, which meant she would have to stay clear of him for a while, even if a part of her yearned to see him again.

Carrying in the last packages from the car, Nan set the bags on the long glass-enclosed counter separating the seating from her prep and serving area. She didn't plan to reopen for a few days but filling the display case and unpacking the cute new teacups and saucers to add to her collection tempted her to flip around the closed sign and lift the shades on the glass door. The inheritance she and Jay had received from both their parents and Nana left them financially free to pursue careers regardless of the salaries. Jay had spoken of going into law enforcement in a large city for as long as she'd thought of nothing but running the tea shop. A pang tightened her abdomen as she recalled the losses that afforded them financial stability at a young age.

She was just finishing setting an array of pastries from the bakery into the refrigerator in the back room and wondering how long news of her return would take to spread when she heard a demanding rap on the front door. "I guess not long," she mumbled with a wry shake of her head. Nan opened the door to her good friend, Tamara Barton, now Dunbar, and took a hasty step back as she pushed her way inside with a gray-eyed glare. "Hey, girlfriend." Nan beamed in welcome, happy to see her again.

"Don't you 'girlfriend' me, Nanette Meyers. You have a lot of explaining to do." Whirling as Nan closed the door, Tamara threw her arms around her for a quick welcome-back hug and then let go to give her another disgruntled look. "Wasn't it just a few months before you took off that you were berating me for being away so long? At least I had the decency to keep in touch."

Nan winced with guilt. "I know, and I'm sorry." Waving a hand toward a table, she said, "Have a seat and I'll brew us some tea."

"Better make enough for several cups. Avery heard of your return at the diner and called Sydney after she talked to me. They'll be here soon." Tamara pulled out a wrought iron chair that matched the quaint, round tables, and plopped down.

Despite the reasons for her long absence and silence, Nan had missed her friends and looked forward to catching up with her and Sydney and Avery. But she could have used a little more time to prepare for their reunion. "You look as if married life agrees with you," she commented, changing the subject as she moved behind the counter. "How is Connor?"

Tamara waved an airy hand. "He's good. Busy with the ranch when he's not tying me up. Seriously, Nan." She leaned her arms on the table with an earnest expression. "Are you all right?"

Looking away to hide the guilt rearing its ugly head, Nan chose a sweet black tea and flipped on one of the brewers. "Yes, and I'm sorry. I shouldn't have stayed away so long."

"Or had your brother return my calls and texts. Why did you?" she persisted, concern lacing her voice.

Shaking her head, Nan dropped individual tea bags into four cups as she heard the door open behind her, followed by Sydney and Avery's voices. Tamara had just moved back to

Willow Springs last year after living in Boise for five years and Nan remembered how put out she'd been when her closest friend refused to tell her why she'd accepted a job so far away. She'd known all her friends would expect an explanation, and she owed them one, but wasn't ready to divulge everything that had happened in New Orleans. All three had embraced the life-style over a year ago, but compared to her experience and needs, they were still newbies. She doubted if any of them, if single, would have sought the diversion of a Dom while away on a short vacation. Nan would pay the price for that mistake for a long time.

"We missed you, and our weekly get-togethers here. Why didn't you tell us you were back?" Sydney asked as Nan turned and carried a tray holding the four steaming cups to the table.

"I'm waiting for an explanation for her silence." Tamara reached for a cup, her eyes staying pinned on Nan as she took a seat next to her.

With a mock frown, Nan berated Avery even though she was at fault for putting off telling them of her return. "You had to go and blab before I got around to calling, didn't you?"

Avery nodded without remorse, blowing on her tea. "Yes. I've got the hang of this small town living now."

"Didn't take you long," Nan muttered. "I'm sorry. I suffered a bad experience I'm not ready to talk about yet, other than to say it has taken me this long to recover enough to come back home. But, God, I really missed you guys."

Worry mingled with curiosity on all three of their faces, but Nan had never been more grateful for their understanding and quiet support when they let it go at that. It helped that each of her friends had, not so long ago, gone through a troubled time and also kept the details to themselves until their guys pried the truth out of them. Luckily for her, no one was interested in her that way, or she in him, to fret about being pushed into revealing her trauma before she was ready.

Avery reached out and squeezed her arm. "We missed you, too, and you know we're here for you when you're ready to talk."

"Thanks for understanding." Avery's large diamond studded wedding band glittered under the light, catching Nan's eye, a reminder of one important event she had missed. After hearing about Tamara and Connor's quick engagement last year, and their plans to hold a double wedding with Sydney and Caden, she hadn't hesitated to postpone her trip for several months to attend. She wouldn't have missed that wedding for anything, but Avery and the sheriff's engagement came after she was already in New Orleans. Missing that special occasion because of her traumatized emotional and physical state was only one of Nan's lingering regrets.

"I'm so sorry I wasn't here for this." She ran a finger over the stunning ring. "All I can say is I was in a bad place, one that has taken me all these months to struggle out of."

"If someone is responsible, give us a name and we'll sic the guys on him." Sydney's teasing tone was at odds with the glint of anger in her green eyes, both expressions warming Nan with gratitude.

Smiling, she relaxed and reached for a cookie. "You know, I just might let you do that sometime, but my brother will insist on getting first crack."

"It must be nice having a close sibling," Avery said on a wistful sigh.

Nan thought of Jay's unyielding support and tireless efforts to get Gerard extradited back to the states after he fled the country when he'd discovered her rescue. She would not have made it through those first grueling months without him. At least she'd been smart enough not to tell Gerard about her brother, the cop.

"It is. But you have someone just as loving and supportive that I don't, so we're even."

Tamara sipped her tea, eying Nan over the dainty china cup. "You could have that too. There were several complaints from the Doms at the club over your absence. They missed you too. Master Dan questioned me several times on whether I had heard from you. You're coming this weekend, aren't you?"

Nan thought of the club she used to love spending weekend nights at, the Masters who were so good at giving her what she craved, dominant men she trusted with her body and who had never let her down or betrayed her feelings. It was no secret the subs favored Master Dan; he enjoyed a reputation for delivering on the promises reflected in his dark eyes. A delicate shiver trickled through her as she recalled praying for his help during those dark, painful days of captivity.

While grappling to hang on to her sanity, she'd taken to conjuring up her favorite scenes from the lifestyle her sexual dissatisfaction had led her into, all of them scenes with the Master who knew her best and she trusted the most. For short periods of time, those memories would sustain her, had kept her mind off the pain and terror she'd endured. Gerard wooed her by promising what she still craved after five plus years of embracing her submissiveness only to strip her of that pleasure by turning into a monster. She lifted a hand to trace over her bare throat. How could she continue to miss something she'd worn for so short a time yet glory in the significance of its absence? Maybe, if she ever came up with an answer as to how she could have been so stupid and trusting and changed her mind about committing to one person, she might solve that question.

Dropping her hand, she noticed her friends' quizzical, troubled faces and rushed to reassure them. "Yeah, I should be able to make it. I'm planning an open house on Saturday but will close by seven. Now, why don't you fill me in on what's been going on around here, and with you guys. Avery, I need to catch up on our book comparisons. I did manage to get quite a few read while I was gone and found some new authors I like." The two of them shared a love of suspense novels and had spent hours discussing books.

Her brown eyes lit with interest. "Me too. The library has been great about ordering anything I request."

"I won't have time this week, but maybe next week we can go over together. Sydney, are you finding your way around here any better?" As Avery and Tamara jumped in to tease Sydney about her penchant for getting lost, the last of Nan's tension melted away. God, she'd really missed them and was glad to be home at last.

The best way to spread the news of her tea shop reopening, Nan knew, was through Dale's Diner. Walking down to the corner on Friday, clutching the flyer she'd made up, she hoped Gertie, the gruff, no-nonsense owner didn't give her too much grief. The widow had a heart of gold but spoke her mind for all to hear. Entering the popular eatery, she cringed as Gertie pierced her with an angry look from behind the counter.

"Hi. I'm back." Nan's wry tone bounced off Gertie, as she'd known it would but still had to try.

"Girl, you've got a lot of explaining to do." Pointing to an empty stool, she snapped, "Sit."

With a rueful shake of her head, Nan crossed the black and white tiled floor, waving to a few people who called out a friendly hello. "I've heard that a lot this week," she admitted as Gertie set a glass of iced tea in front of her.

After a silent moment enduring the older woman's careful scrutiny, Gertie replied, "Landed yourself into some trouble." She nodded and slapped a menu down. "Good thing you got your butt back where it belongs. Today's on the house. We're out of meatloaf."

"Order up, Gert!" Clyde, the head cook called out, lifting his hand and smiling at Nan. "Welcome back."

"Thanks, Clyde." Nan watched Gertie stomp over to the open shelf where he'd placed two steaming plates.

Picking them up, she tossed back at Nan, "Be right back, so don't dally deciding what you want. I'm busy."

God, it's so damn good to be home. At least, she thought so until a deep voice she knew well said from behind her, "That old woman hasn't changed, has she?"

Dan Shylock slid onto the stool next to her and Nan stiffened in immediate awareness. As happy as she was with the sweeping, familiar warm rush of pleasure his nearness and deep tenor always produced, she needed to be very careful. His astuteness as both a Dom and a friend who knew her well meant she needed to school her features carefully before she dared look up into those dark, compelling eyes again.

Nan huffed a small laugh, shaking her head. "No, she hasn't, thank God." Taking a deep breath, she turned and smiled. His tipped Stetson shadowed his tanned face, but she could still see the curve of his lips and the sharp, assessing look in those dark brown eyes. "Neither have you. Hi there. Long time, no see," she quipped, keeping it as light and casual as possible considering the way her stomach cramped with worry over what he might see that she wasn't ready for.

Dan cocked his head and took his time looking Nan over, his welcome smile slipping as he glimpsed a wariness reflected in her honey-gold gaze she'd never exhibited toward him before. The new shadows under her eyes and pinched tightness around her soft mouth set off his inner alarm. The woman and submissive he'd known for several years had looked at him with teasing flirtation, strong-willed independence and lustful need, but never with such a guarded expression, as if she were trying to keep something from him. It both hurt and pissed him off almost as much as her long absence followed by her return without a word from her.

"Yes, too long." Removing his hat, he ran a hand through his shoulder-length blond hair, noticing the extra inches of her sable tresses. He liked the way the ends curled around her shoulders but would miss sifting his fingers through the shorter strands as he cupped her scalp. "I was on my way to see you when I spotted you coming in here. No offense, hon, but you don't appear as if your time away agreed with you."

His Dom radar went on high alert when she shifted her gaze away from him, her fingers toying with the silverware in front of her. "I had issues to deal with is all." She shrugged, the gesture as evasive as her answer and unlike the outgoing woman he knew who didn't shy away from anything or anyone.

"You couldn't do that without cutting yourself off from everyone?" he prodded, dissatisfied with the vague reply.

Nan tensed before glancing back at him with a familiar look of determination. "No," she returned succinctly, "I couldn't."

"I'm sorry to hear that." And Dan was. He'd always held an extra fondness for Nan, ever since he'd noticed the gleam of interest and expectation on her face when the Master training her had released her to explore her submissive needs with others. He'd been the first to snatch her up for a scene and the two of them had been dancing to the same tune until she'd left for a short vacation and stayed away for far longer than planned without an explanation to anyone.

For years Dan had cherished the comfortable fit of their unique, two-sided relationship. The occasional Dom/sub scene they indulged in had never interfered with the casual friendship they'd developed away from the sex-charged club atmosphere. She embraced sexual dominance with cock-hardening submissiveness but maintained her fierce independence outside the club and possessed an admirable streak of loyalty toward her friends. Those traits were a perfect fit for what they both wanted out of a relationship but were also what made her silence these many months and the changes he could see on her face suspect. For the first time since he'd known her, he found himself struggling against the urge to go all Dom on her here, in public and outside the club, to demand answers she didn't want to give.

"Dan, didn't see you come in. May as well take your order too," Gertie said, her sudden appearance dispelling the awkward moment between him and Nan.

They both ordered the cheeseburger and fries, only he added a shake with his. He noticed the flyer advertising her re-opening right before she held it up for Gertie. "Do you mind if I put this on your bulletin board, Gertie?" she asked.

"You know I don't, girl. I'll even send them down the street after they come in here. We'll get you back up and in business in no time."

Her face softened with her smile. "Thanks."

"That's what friends do around here, be there for each other. You'd do well to remember that." Gertie turned and called out to the kitchen, "Two cheeseburgers and fries," without pausing as she stomped down to the other end of the counter.

"Looks like I'm not the only one unhappy with your long, unexplained absence." Unable to resist, Dan pinched her chin and turned her face toward him, holding her there even though her eyes darkened with annoyance and she tried to jerk free. "In case you've forgotten, you can come to me with anything, tell me anything. I don't judge, you know that, or you should." He released her and changed the subject as her expression turned rigid. "I have a new foal, born seven months ago. Pretty little filly. You'll have to come out and see her sometime."

Nan's face lost her rigid irritation and her eyes lit with interest, a familiar look it relieved him to see. She loved horses, and he knew she'd always wanted one of her own, but not until she could buy enough acres to stable it herself. That was part of her independent streak that right now was causing her to remain mute on her reasons for staying away.

"I'd love to." Her rigid shoulders relaxed with the eagerness in her eyes. "Thanks. Maybe next week, after I get the shop going again. Are you still working with military parolees?"

"Sure, just let me know, and yes, I hired two new guys several months ago." The troubled vets used the time, space and work he offered to transition back into civilian life and acclimate themselves to their freedom from both drugs and prison before returning to their loved ones or heading out on their own. Of the previous eight men he'd sponsored, only one had lapsed bad enough he'd ended up back on drugs.

Gertie returned with their orders and Dan shoved aside his curiosity and concern to savor spending time with Nan again. The instant rush of excitement upon seeing her again felt damned good, his relief when Connor called to tell him she was back palpable. Even though he itched to get to the bottom of her trouble, he refrained from pushing too hard. He'd run up against the brick wall of her stubborn independence before and didn't relish starting their reunion on a negative note.

They spoke of everything except about the months she was away and the reason for her extended visit. By the time they finished their lunch, they had rekindled their easy friendship, enjoying it almost as much as before she'd left. His impatience to discover what happened that caused those shadows under her eyes was his only regret as he stood to leave. With luck, once she submitted to him again at the club, he would be successful in getting those answers.

He tossed down a generous tip and reached out to give her hair an affectionate tug, something he'd done countless times before, only to have her jerk away, as if fearing that small prick on her scalp instead of relishing it. Her face whitened and then flushed, the uncharacteristic response heightening his suspicion something dire was going on with her.

Nan slid off the stool, backing away, her retreat a painful kick to his gut. "Sorry. I…"

Dan laid a firm finger over her lips. "Don't say anything unless it's the truth." Dropping his hand, he wasn't surprised at the mulish set of her mouth or her silence. Sighing in disappointment, he said, "I hope you'll join us at the club tonight. We've missed you."

Shaking her head, she replied, "I don't have time, but should tomorrow night."

He nodded and turned to leave. "See you tomorrow then."

She waited until he'd taken two steps away before saying, "I've missed you, too, and everyone else."

He swiveled his head to look at her as he settled his hat back on and nodded. "Good to know."

———

Nan sat back down, nibbling on the last of her fries as she watched Dan walk out of the diner, her heart executing a funny roll she didn't know how to decipher. She'd always been attracted to men wearing a Stetson, cowboy boots and tight jeans. Dan's six-foot-two lean build was a good match for her five-foot-eight slender body and his strict dominance suited her sexual needs. Or, at least it used to. Now, she didn't know what she liked or wanted, other than to get her life back. She knew returning to The Barn played a crucial role in succeeding, but when he brought it up, she'd gone cold thinking about it. That both depressed her and pissed her off.

She left Gertie a generous tip and took her time strolling back to the tea shop to soak up the mid-afternoon sun, missing the low hum of arousal she used to experience whenever she would spend time with the town's sexy lawyer. Seven years ago, rumors had spread like wildfire about the good-looking attorney who opened a law practice after buying a small spread nearby. He'd been new to the club the same time as she, but unlike her, was already an experienced player in the lifestyle. She'd noticed him around Willow Springs and fantasized about submitting to him during her instruction phase whenever she would catch him eying her scenes with Master Clayton. One look from those chocolate eyes had never failed to divert her attention and send her blood pumping in a molten flow of heat.

Until today. Nan's response to seeing Dan again had been tepid compared to the instant hot feedback she'd always experienced in the past and was just one more thing she blamed on Gerard and vowed to overcome. That son-of-a-bitch had robbed her of enough time and sanity. Stepping inside her shop, the warm sense of being home washed over her, bolstering her determination to move forward without the fear constantly looking back evoked.

Saturday flew by as a steady stream of customers, new and old, came in to welcome Nan home and express their happiness at her reopening. She worked with tireless energy to fill orders and ring up sales while answering questions and relaying her appreciation, all the while wondering how she could have let herself forget how much friendship meant. The weeks of recovery and months of waiting out the legal battle to extradite Gerard back to the states after he'd fled to Canary Island had beaten down what little of her self-esteem remained after Jay freed her from his depravity. She was still waging the battle to get it back, to bolster the courage that aided in getting her home and that was mandatory to overcome her trauma completely.

But today helped, and she intended to capitalize on her upbeat mood and energy to prepare for a visit to The Barn in a few hours. At fifteen minutes before closing, the bell on the door pealed again and Willa Hoyt, the librarian for as long as Nan could remember, entered with another older woman.

"Willa." Nan beamed at the woman who had been a regular pinochle player with her grandmother. "How are you?"

"Oh, I'm fine, Nanette." Coming up to the counter, she looked Nan over with a critical eye. "You look good. Lordy, girl, I've missed you, and coming in here for my afternoon tea."

Nan hurried around the counter and hugged the teary-eyed woman who, she knew, wasn't as frail as she appeared. "I'm sorry. There were issues keeping me tied up in Louisiana, extending my stay longer than I'd planned." Pulling back, she smiled at her companion. "And who is this?"

"Alice Juneu, my new, part-time volunteer. She's agreed to drive in from Billings twice a week to help me out so I can keep working. Isn't that wonderful?"

"It is," Nan agreed, holding her hand out to Alice. "It's nice to meet you. How about a cup of tea and a scone from the bakery on the house?"

"That sounds lovely, dear." Alice squeezed her hand with a grip that belied her petite stature. A soft smile eased the cold scrutiny in her eyes and Nan figured she was being protective of her new friend. She couldn't fault her for that. "I just happened to meet Willa at the librarian luncheon in Billings and we hit it off."

"Well, as a frequent patron, I appreciate you volunteering. The library wouldn't be the same without Willa there. I'll have to come over soon and check out the new releases. I never could get into e-book reading. Do you still like mint, Willa?" Nan shuffled back behind the counter and grabbed two of her prettiest teacups and saucers.

"I do, thank you, but I see you were about to close. Why don't you pour them in to-go cups? We can visit more when you come to the library."

"Nonsense. I have time and I know you'll enjoy being the first to sip from these delicate china cups I brought back from New Orleans. Have a seat."

"Did you have a nice vacation in Louisiana?" Alice asked as they sat down.

The only other patrons still occupying a table rose and waved to Nan as the two women left. "Thanks for coming in," she called out as she worked to get her emotions in check. Alice's innocent referral to her time in New Orleans as a vacation stirred up her resentment with the memories. What was supposed to be a pleasant vacation had turned into a nightmare, but no one here knew that.

"Let's just say I'm in no hurry to go back."

Chapter 3

Riding high on the success of her open house, Nan flipped the closed sign around after Willa and Alice left and then trotted upstairs to get ready for her first night out in way too long. Regardless of the misgivings plaguing her since her uncharacteristic, negative reaction to Dan yesterday, she was still determined to overcome any and all obstacles in her path to regaining the pleasures she used to relish about the BDSM lifestyle. Maybe the fastest route to the end would be to jump into a scene with the first Dom who invited her, she mused as she stepped into the shower.

Propping one foot on the corner seat, she lathered her pubic hair and swiped a razor over her pubis. Despite the heat building in the small cubicle, she broke out in a nauseous sweat as she exposed that sensitive skin for the first time in eight months. Setting her jaw, she refused to let yet another negative response deter her. For years, she'd kept a standing, monthly spa appointment in Billings that included a wax job of her pubic hair, but the pleasure of keeping herself denuded was only one of the things Gerard's abuse had stripped her of. She gritted her teeth as she lifted the handheld showerhead and rinsed the suds and hair away. Instead of the prickles of heightened sensation she expected to experience, the memory of how he'd gripped the soft, bare folds and squeezed until she screamed rushed to the surface.

Goddamn it, I won't go there, Nan swore, forcing herself to maintain the pelting spray aimed between her legs until the painful memory slipped away. A few moments later, she released her pent-up breath as her roiling stomach settled back down and the shivers ceased. Flipping off the water, she brushed her fingers across the newly exposed flesh, proud of herself for putting mind over matter as the dormant sensations of the past months tingled to life under her light touch. Still shy of what she used to feel, the pleasant shivers nevertheless gave her the small rush of pleasure and boost of courage she needed so much.

Baby steps, sis. Promise me you'll take it slow when you return to your club. Jay's words played through Nan's head as she dried off and padded naked into her bedroom to search for something to wear. She knew she should go slow and had promised her brother she would. But frustration and a long-denied ache kept pushing her to get going, to hightail it out to the secluded, renovated barn and latch on to the first Dom who caught her eye before she changed her mind. Or the memories could change it for her.

As she flipped through the fetish clothes and lingerie she was so fond of, she knew she wouldn't be wearing any of them. Nan hadn't shied away from public exposure since her first few nights under Master Clayton's tutelage, but she also hadn't been naked in front of anyone since her rescuers had covered her bloodied, abused body upon her rescue. She couldn't expose her scars until her friends knew about Gerard and she was prepared to answer questions. With longing, she recalled the illicit thrill of wearing the leather corsets that exposed her nipples and the thongs that drew eyes to her butt, the excitement of being stripped, or ordered to strip off a sexy teddy in front of others, of loving their eyes on her nudity.

Maybe not tonight, but she'd get all of that back, somehow, someway. Tonight would start the journey.

Nan settled on a short, snug white leather skirt and silky, sapphire tee. Goosebumps raced across her skin as the supple leather stretched over her buttocks left bare by a white thong and the soft silk caressed her braless nipples. After leaving on several lights, both inside and out, she slid behind the wheel of her sporty Nissan. Ignoring the steady rapid beat of her heart as she drove down the highway, she tightened her hands on the wheel and made the turn onto the narrow, unpaved road that led to The Barn.

By the time she parked in the tree-shrouded copse, her sweat-slicked hands were white-knuckled with her taut grip. She gazed with longing at the familiar structure, the wide double doors and the large, upper window with its faint yellow glow. She wanted to rush inside and see everyone again, to hear the sounds of play resonating and smell the pungent odor of leather mingling with sex so bad she could taste it. But still, she sat there.

Another car pulled in and Nan watched Master Brett open the door for his wife, Sue Ellen. The petite blonde leaned into her husband and there was no mistaking the look of yearning, excitement and contentment reflected on her face. He clasped her nape and kissed her, long and hard, his free hand sliding down to grip her left buttock.

The ache settling between Nan's legs spread to her chest and propelled her out of the car to follow the couple inside. "Hey, you two. How are you?"

Master Brett smiled in welcome as he held open the door. "Nan, it's good to see you back. We're doing fine. You?"

"Happy to be home. Sue Ellen, I love the dress." Nan eyed the slinky satin sheath held on by two, thin ties at the shoulders with envy.

"Thanks. Master Brett surprised me with it tonight. I'm sorry I didn't make it to your open house today," she said as they both slipped off their shoes and stowed them in cubicles under Master Brett's watchful eye. "I promise I'll come by this week."

"I'll look forward to it." Nan's throat closed up as Master Brett opened the door into the playroom and a lifestyle she craved to embrace again. She waved the couple off as she scanned the tables between her and the center-placed bar for her friends, praying for the sudden inner quaking of her body to cease.

As she stood rooted where she was, she didn't understand the hesitancy and nerves assailing her. Unlike the BDSM mixer where she'd met Gerard, she knew these people. They were friends, both the men and women, some she'd known for decades, others since they'd become members. They weren't strangers plotting to seduce, kidnap and traumatize her. They were people she cared about, and who cared for her, whom she could trust to be herself. They had nothing in common with the man she'd been foolish enough to fall for every lie and conniving suggestion out of his mouth.

Nan spotted Tamara and Sydney seated at the bar and when Tamara waved her over, she forced her leaden feet to move. Her gaze shifted up to the dimly lit loft, and the apparatus she favored being bound to the last time she was here. Longing and fear battled for supremacy inside her head as she wound through the tables and seating areas, pasting on a smile and returning greetings she hoped hid the turmoil raging inside her.

"I was starting to think you weren't going to show tonight," Tamara greeted her as Nan slid onto the stool next to her.

"Sorry, a few last-minute customers kept me late and then I had to get ready. Hey, Caden. Do you have a beer for me?" She found it easy to smile at Sydney's husband, a local rancher who had grown up in Willow Springs the same as she but was years ahead of her in school. He still wore his Stetson, but she could make out enough of his rough-hewn face and blue eyes to see he hadn't changed since their wedding.

"Damn, it's good to see you again, Nan." Reaching across the bar, he cupped the back of her head and drew her forward for a quick kiss. "We heard you were back," he said after releasing her and grabbing a cold bottle from under the counter.

"I hadn't planned on being away so long and I've missed you guys, and this place."

"It wasn't the same without you, Nan." Sydney lifted her beer in a toast to her return.

Nan smiled down at her, noticing the nipple huggers adorning her breasts through the thin tank she wore. It was easy to conjure up the pleasure those clamps could wreak despite the length of time since she'd worn a pair and recalled how effective they were in making her tips throb and ache for more. "You look like you've gotten along fine without me but tell me. How many times did you get lost while I was gone?" Sydney's poor sense of direction landed her on the club's doorstep instead of at the Dunbar Ranch over a year ago, where she was due to report for her new job as their cook. She met her boss, Caden, only neither knew it at the time he confronted her spying in the window.

"Ha, ha. I've been finding my way around now for some time, as I told you the other day."

Caden handed Nan a beer, smirking at his wife. "Didn't I have to come find you just yesterday when you went riding with Tamara and got turned around coming back to our place?"

"I gave you explicit directions," Tamara said, surprised. "How'd you manage to get turned around?"

Sydney shrugged, unconcerned. "I'm good at it. Besides, you didn't say anything about that pond. That threw me off." Shifting on the barstool, she groaned and glared at Caden. "Wasn't the spanking enough? You had to use the plug, too?"

"That reminds me. As soon as Connor arrives, I need to remove it. But since you've been so good, I'll make sure you enjoy it."

Sydney sighed, her green eyes going soft as she watched her husband saunter down the bar to serve someone else.

"Quit looking like that, Syd. My Master isn't here yet," Tamara groused, but with a small smile curving her mouth.

Nan laughed, her initial tension easing the longer she sat there surrounded by friends. Good memories assailed her for a change as she listened to the teasing banter and sipped her beer as music, low conversations and laughter resonated around the room.

"Where is Connor?" she asked Tamara. "I'm surprised he's not glued to your side."

"He and Jason, you remember my foreman, went to an auction in Bozeman, so he's running late. Amy and I spent the day shopping in Billings, looking for her dress. Oh, I forgot to tell you. My stepmother and Jason are getting married in a few weeks."

"That was… is great. I'm happy for them." She was about to say that was fast, but that news was just another reminder of how long she'd been away.

Taking another swig of the cold brew, Nan let her eyes wander around the room and spotted Master Greg and Master Devin on the dance floor, a tall blonde sandwiched between their gyrating bodies. The best friends were already enjoying a reputation for indulging in ménages the last time she'd been here, and it appeared they still did as she watched Greg reach around and cup the woman's naked breasts, lifting them for Devin's descending mouth. Heat curled low in her belly as Greg flipped up the girl's skirt and ground his denim covered pelvis against her bare ass while Devin slid a hand between her legs and tugged on one, turgid nipple.

"God, they are so freakin' hot." Sydney sighed, fanned herself and then took a long drink from her amber filled glass. "You were with them once, weren't you, Nan?"

"Yes, and yes, it was as good as you would think watching

them." Nan shifted as her pussy softened and dampened, the response surprising her. She hadn't felt an ounce of arousal in so long, she'd despaired of ever getting the pleasant feeling back.

"I've never indulged in a three-way. I wonder if Connor…" Tamara squealed when hard hands plucked her off the stool and brought her up against her husband's tall frame. "Oh, hi." She flipped him a sheepish grin with a toss of her midnight hair.

"If *Master* Connor would what? Let someone else touch you? No fucking way, sweetie." Lifting his head, he tipped his hat back and his small grin spread into a wide smile as he looked at Nan. "Damn, it's good to see you again." Keeping one hand on Tamara, he leaned over and pinched Nan's chin, tilting her face up for a quick kiss, much like his brother greeted her with. Releasing her, he cocked his head and a glint appeared in his blue eyes, "I think I recall a number of Doms promising retribution for your long, *silent* absence."

Nan winced, her tension returning, and knew Master Connor thought it was because of his emphasis on silent, not the thought of a Dom's retribution. She used to respond without hesitation when a Master hinted at punishment and to the idea of a long, over-the-knee, bare-butt spanking with excitement and longing. Before she'd left, everyone here knew how much she enjoyed the bite of pain, and the pleasure it always led to. But that was before Gerard showed her what real agony was, how deep the pain could go, how devastating, mind-numbing and terrorizing it could be.

Nan chugged the beer, looking away from Connor's keen, appraising gaze as suspicion clouded his eyes. The cold against her palm helped steady her under his probing look, the long pull she took of the alcohol aided in calming the sudden jitters tightening her abdomen. Swallowing, she lowered the bottle and released an exasperated huff. "I guess I've got that coming, but give me tonight to just settle back in, would you?"

Caden frowned as he strolled up in time to hear their

exchange, his gaze shifting behind her as he drawled, "What do you think, Master Dan?"

Nan stiffened, something close to panic threatening her composure. Tamara reached out and squeezed her arm, her and Sydney seeing more than she wanted them to from the looks of sympathy and puzzlement on their faces.

"I think the sub I remember would have vibrated with excitement at the mention of punishment and jumped to embrace the prospect."

That deep voice, the only one to slither past the fear and pain numbing her mind during three days of huddling in cold, complete darkness, now drew a wave of rippling uncertainty. After taking another long drink, she swiveled to face Dan, leaned forward with a small grin and managed to pull up the old Nan still struggling to re-emerge.

"Master Dan. For you, I might change my mind."

Apparently, she wouldn't make a good actress. His narrowed dark eyes and tight set to his mouth signaled he saw through her attempt to flirt with and tease with him. She didn't like the calculated gleam that entered his eyes as he removed his hat and tossed it on the bar top. He fisted his hands on his hips, drawing her gaze to the thick, wide belt around his waist and she recalled the sting of the supple leather snapping across her buttocks. The quick, welcome rush of heat subsided as he held out his hand, a silent invitation he'd issued, and she'd accepted, countless times before.

Nan started to reach for him, ignoring the churning in her gut, determined to move forward no matter what, when the sudden *whoosh* and snap of leather striking bare skin followed by a high-pitched screech echoed down from the loft and pitched her back into that dark space where the same sound had delivered waves of excruciating agony. Bile pushed up to clog her throat and freeze her acceptance of Master Dan's offer. She squeezed her eyes shut, the only way to keep from looking up at the source of another flesh-connecting snap. Jerking as if struck, the memory of searing pain splitting her skin and blood dripping swept back to haunt her.

"Breathe, Nan." Master Dan emphasized that command by pushing her head down and massaging the tight muscles of her upper back.

She fought the swell of despair and humiliation as hard as she struggled to breathe in. *I'm still as much of a pathetic mess as I was months ago*. The thought pissed her off as fast as that sound hurled her back to a place she never wanted to go again.

"Nan, are you okay?"

The soft concern lacing Tamara's voice and Dan's soothing touch broke through the final dredges of icy blackness threatening to keep her prisoner back in that horrible time. Nan sucked in a deep breath and nodded, pushing against Dan's hand as she strained to rise. He removed it without hesitation and she lifted up, clenching her hands and jaw until her bearings steadied.

"Sorry," she croaked, forcing a self-conscious laugh as she reached for the beer again. "I guess I'm still exhausted from traveling and the busy week of getting the shop re-opened. *Whew!*" She drew an exaggerated hand sweep across her brow and took a fortifying, guzzling drink that emptied the bottle. "It's going to have to be an early night for me, I'm afraid." Forcing herself to look up at Master Dan, she tried not to react to his scowl as she asked, "Raincheck?"

He nodded, reaching for her elbow as she slid off the stool. "I'll hold you to it. Come on, I'll walk you out."

Shaken by her reaction, especially after feeling so good and positive, Nan pulled away from Master Dan's grasp and turned her back on his astute, watchful gaze. "Thanks, but I'm fine. Catch you guys later."

He caught up with her halfway to the front doors and she stiffened as he took her arm again. "I insist," he stated in a cool, rigid tone she knew well.

Annoyance with both herself and him rose to the surface, shoving aside the remnants of her mortification. "Look," she snapped, rounding on him as he opened the door to the foyer, "I didn't agree to scene with you, so back off." Yanking her arm free, she strode to the wall of cubbies and grabbed her sandals.

"I'm well aware of that, Nan, but I would be remiss in my responsibilities if I let any sub leave when upset without assuring she was all right to drive."

A muscle ticced in his cheek, drawing her eyes to his taut, five o'clock shadowed jaw. She'd always found the contrast between his sandy blond hair and dark eyes and face as attractive as his hard Dom persona here at the club. It was another blow to her resolve to get her life back that she wasn't pulsating with needful lust to submit to her favorite Master's strict dominance.

Looking down to slip on her shoes, she managed to return in a steady voice, "I'm not upset, just tired. As I said, it's been an exhausting week of trying to catch up." Straightening, she pasted on a calm expression and prayed he didn't see her still jumpy nerves. "I may have been away for a while, but I've driven home from this place plenty of times after an intense night of play without a problem. A little fatigue will not hinder my driving. Good night, Master Dan."

Nan made it the few steps to the front door and grasped the handle before he asked a question she wasn't prepared to answer. "Who hurt you, Nan?"

She didn't dare turn around; he would be sure to see the revealing shock reflected on her face. Damn it, what made her believe she was ready to return tonight, to face the Doms who knew her best and would be sure to see more than she wanted, than she was ready for anyone to see? Shaking her head, she walked away as calmly as possible considering her racing heart, feeling his eyes on her as she got into her car and drove away without a backward glance.

Dan waited in the open doorway until Nan's taillights disappeared from view, suspicion forming a cold knot of dread in his gut. The way her face turned sheet-white upon hearing the strike of Master Devin's single tail hand whip and Mindy's cry had taken him aback. There had been an indefinable panicked flash in her gold eyes that caused him a moment of dread before he took control and pushed her head down. Her excuse of fatigue sounded reasonable, but somehow rang with the hint of evasion, as proven by the way she kept looking away from him. He remembered how she pulled back with a startled jerk when he'd gone to tug on her hair at the diner and didn't like where his thoughts were going.

Nan was an experienced sub, he reminded himself as he returned inside with different scenarios of possible reasons for her uncharacteristic reactions running through his head, none of which sat right with him. She liked the bite of pain and where it led her, and all but begged for a rough fuck whenever they took a scene that far. But even so, he couldn't imagine her allowing a Dom to go further than she was comfortable with. She was flirtatiously open and brazen, never holding back or shying away from what she wanted, and she was just as delightful when she rebuked a pushy man who didn't interest her or in ending a scene that was either not enough or leaning toward too much. At least, she had been before going to New Orleans.

One thing was clear, he decided as his head pounded with the urge to get answers, something significant had happened that kept her away so long and put that look on her face. The question was, what?

"What happened?" Tamara pounced as soon as he reached them, worry darkening her gray eyes. "Is Nan okay? I should have been there to help her more this week."

"She appeared to be by the time she left." *Appeared* being the operative word. "But our girl has come home with some issues. Maybe you can get her to open up more about her time away, Tamara. Give me a double, Caden, would you?"

"I'll join you in one," he replied with an edge to his tone and concern swirling in his blue eyes Dan could commiserate with.

Connor hugged Tamara against him. "Her reaction was odd, given her experience. It's not like she's not familiar with the sights and sounds going on around here. Maybe it's just the length of time she's been away from the lifestyle combined with, like she said, the long week."

That made sense, Dan admitted, so why was he mentally dismissing Connor's suggestion? Ten months was a long time for a woman who embraced her submissiveness with such whole-hearted acceptance and enthusiasm to go without getting her needs met. He hoped her craving for sexual release through submission hadn't led her into a bad situation with the wrong person.

Tamara cut a quick glance toward Sydney, who seemed as worried about their friend as she was. "We'll talk to her, but if Nan doesn't want to reveal anything, or not yet, we have to respect that." She pinned Dan with a direct gaze. "We *all* have to respect her privacy, if she wishes to hold on to it for now."

Under any other circumstances, likely with any other woman, Dan would agree with Tamara. But his relationship with Nan included a long-standing friendship that surpassed them indulging in occasional play here at The Barn. He would try for patience, but if she continued with the odd behavior that reeked of a trauma he needed to know about before he could avail himself of that slender, curvy body again, he would insist on answers sooner rather than later.

"Of course," he replied as smoothly as the last swallow of whiskey went down his throat. Setting the glass on the bar top, he nodded at the Dunbars. "I'll head up and relieve Grayson and catch you later."

"I like your openness, and the way you don't shy away from what you want, and need." Gerard's black eyes glittered with appreciation as he swept Nan's body from head to toe. Reaching out, he traced one finger in a circle around her right nipple, the light touch through the thin halter top enough to draw the tender bud into a tight pucker.

"It's difficult to get those needs met if I don't embrace them," Nan admitted candidly, her pussy heating as he gripped her nape and held her head immobile as he took possession of her mouth. The man kissed as good as he looked, she mused, loving his tight hold and the hard pressure of his lips moving over hers. The wild beat of her pulse and escalating ache between her legs that had begun the moment she entered the BDSM mixer and spotted the tall, midnight-haired Dom from across the room obliterated the low murmurs of conversations going on around them.

"Let's take this back to my place," he suggested after releasing her mouth, his hand squeezing her neck.

Nan groaned and rolled over in bed, tensing against the dream forcing its way past her subconscious against her will. The last thing she needed was a nightmare-inducing memory sabotaging her much-desired sleep. She tried to think about something else, someone else to keep it at bay. Closing her eyes again, Master Dan's face swam into her head and she warmed as she always did when she thought about her favorite Dom. But as she drifted back to sleep, the pleasure she always experienced whenever he gave her one of his pointed, heated looks changed to a shiver of cold trepidation as the past intruded with ruthless insistency and Master Gerard's cold, dark face returned to haunt her.

"On your knees, slave," Master Gerard barked, his sudden tight grip of Nan's wrists and shove to the cold, concrete floor wrenching a cry from her.

Gritting her teeth, she glared up at him, wondering what she had gotten herself into. Gone was the friendly Dom she met a few days ago who had been courting her submissive surrender with experienced, body humming enticements; now replaced by a ruthless son-of-a-bitch whose current expression gave her the willies.

"I'm no man's slave and never agreed to that role. Let. Me. Go."

Before she could fathom his intention, he swung his free hand and backhanded her, his hold tightening, keeping her from toppling back. Pain exploded across her face and blood filled her mouth as shock rendered her speechless for several breathless moments.

Oh, God, *she groaned in silent, escalating fear,* what have I gotten myself into?

Nan jerked awake, her heart pounding hard enough to burst through her chest as she blinked against the bright swath of sunlight streaming through the open shades and covering her bed. The warmth helped push back the cold terror still shaking her insides, but she despaired of anything helping her enough to overcome the worst mistake she'd ever made.

Chapter 4

"God, yes," Nan muttered as she glanced at the text Tamara sent her, asking if she wanted to go riding after she closed today. After her sleepless night and the long afternoon of serving and socializing with her customers, she was more than ready for fresh air and the joy of an invigorating, mind-clearing run with her best friend. Her favorite activity since childhood, she'd missed horseback riding this past year, the euphoric rush of a powerful animal's muscles straining under her as they flew across the wide-open prairie grasslands brightened with summer foliage, the afternoon sun beating down on her back. She'd been so cold for so long despite spending the winter in New Orleans' balmy temperatures instead of the harsher, frigid Montana months.

Sending an affirmative reply, she finished wiping down the counter as she scanned the few remaining customers still lingering. It had been the right move adding gourmet coffees to the menu, as the line forming an hour before her regular opening time proved. Stumbling downstairs this morning, praying she'd masked the dark circles under her eyes well enough, the smiling, eager faces waiting to come in had heartened her. At least she wasn't a failure in everything, she thought, switching off the kettles and waving goodbye to the last people leaving. Only when it came to regaining enough confidence to let go, like she used to, at the club. Every time she took a step, her silk panties glided over the newly exposed, sensitive flesh of her labia, a constant reminder how she'd failed the first step toward getting her life back in order, each nerve tingling caress a taunt about her cowardice.

"Don't get discouraged," Jay told her when he'd skyped this morning and zeroed in on her distraught, tired features. "It was your first time back. Cut yourself some slack and don't push it."

Like everything else since her ordeal, that was easier said than done, and patience wasn't her strong suit when it came to wallowing in self-pity. Her brother's unconditional support meant the world to her, but, damn it, physically she was more than ready to pick up the satisfying sex life she'd enjoyed before Gerard stripped her of the pleasure she used to reap from pain. If only her head would get on board with her body, then life could return to normal.

An hour later, Nan pulled onto the Barton property and parked in front of the ranch home where Tamara's stepmother now resided with her soon-to-be husband and their foreman, Jason. Sliding out of her car, a high-pitched neigh drew her attention to the stables. Tethered at the rail fencing in a small, attached corral, Tamara's Arabian stallion, Galahad tossed his gray/white head and long mane. Standing next to him, saddled and ready to go, stood Lady, a pretty dappled mare appearing just as eager for a run.

Nan headed their way, waving as Tamara came out of the stables. "Thanks for the invitation." Reaching the horses, she ran a hand down Lady's sleek neck. "Aren't you a pretty girl?" she crooned. "She doesn't act as timid as the last time I saw her."

"I've been working with her, and Galahad's enthusiastic acceptance has helped. I think he's going to be a daddy next year." Excitement shone in Tamara's eyes as she pushed to her toes and looked at Nan over the backs of both horses. "And Connor and I are trying our best to beat her to it."

Nan's small grin split into a wide smile. "No shit? You two are wasting no time making up for lost time." Connor's resistance to change their relationship from friends to lovers had driven everyone crazy.

Tamara swung up into the saddle, lifting a slim brow as Nan followed suit and settled on top of Lady. "We're coming up on our first anniversary already, remember?"

"Is that your not-so-subtle way of reminding me how long I stayed away?"

"Yes. We can talk about that or your sudden dizzy spell last night." Nudging Galahad into a slow walk, she glanced over as Nan steered Lady alongside her. "Or why you look so wiped out today, as if you haven't slept."

Nan lightly poked Lady's sides with her heels, prodding her into a trot as they reached the field. "Or," she tossed over her shoulder, "we can just enjoy the afternoon in silence."

The faster gait whipped her hair around her face, snapping the dark brown strands against her neck and cheeks. She'd always kept her hair short, liking the extra burn against her scalp that came from a Dom needing a firmer grip to hold on that wasn't necessary with longer hair. That small pleasure was just another thing Gerard had stolen from her when he dragged her across the cement floor by her short hair, drawing blood as he pulled it out by the roots. With a shudder of queasy remembrance, she leaned over Lady's neck and kicked her into a ground-covering run.

The sun beat down on her back, the warmth pushing back the ever-present cold as they raced across the field. She laughed as Tamara pulled ahead of her with a taunting grin, the little mare no match for her friend's stallion. But Nan didn't care. It was enough to bask in the freedom of traversing the wide-open range dotted with grazing cattle, the prairie grasses brightened with a smattering of pink bitterroot and yellow coneflower summer blossoms. By the time they reached the fence line separating the Barton ranch from the Dunbar's, they were laughing with the exuberance of silly teens, their chests heaving from the physical effort it had taken to keep their seats during such a rigorous ride.

"No fair," Nan panted, pulling up on the reins to slow Lady down as they approached Tamara at the fence. "If you'd paired me with a horse comparable in size and stamina, I would have had a shot at beating you."

Tamara shrugged and leaned down to pat Galahad's neck. "He doesn't like being far away from his girl, so suck it up." The rapid pounding of clomping hooves drew both their gazes over the fence at the approaching riders and Tamara's smile stretched even wider.

"Shit, girlfriend," Nan drawled with a shake of her head, "can't he let you out of his sight for more than an hour?"

"Nope, and I love it." Tamara laughed as Nan rolled her eyes. "Someday you'll see why."

"Why what?" Connor asked, pulling to a stop and tipping his hat back to level a hot, blue-eyed look on his wife.

Dan rode up beside him as Tamara replied, "Why I like being your girl."

Connor grinned. "This commitment stuff does come with some perks, doesn't it, sweetie?"

Nan glanced at Dan, the sudden tenseness that gripped her when she'd seen him riding up easing as he winked and the corner of his mouth kicked up in a wry grin. "Not as many as staying footloose and fancy free, right, Nan?"

"That's always been my intention."

The last crumbs of the sleepless night and tiring day fell away as he greeted her with the usual congeniality the two of them had always reverted to when not at the club. After he'd shown his displeasure over her months of silence and his suspicion of her odd behavior last night, she wondered how he'd react when he saw her again. She knew her friends questioned how she could maintain a casual friendship with a man she regularly submitted her sexual needs to but switching back and forth between the roles of Dom/sub and good friends had always been easy for the two of them.

That didn't keep Nan from admiring how his lean, muscled body looked astride his large, gorgeous Appaloosa or responding to the noticeable tightening of his thighs gripping the animal's heaving sides and the dark slash of his gaze from under the sexy brim of his lowered Stetson. Her girly parts certainly sat up and took notice, the pucker of her nipples accompanying the quick spasm clutching her pussy. That welcome response offered her hope the lapse into the past she suffered last night wouldn't return the next time. To play it safe, though, maybe she should take up with another Dom, one who didn't know her as well, or who wasn't as astute as her friend and occasional Master.

"Have you finished your rounds?" Tamara asked.

"Yep, and Sydney instructed us to fetch you for dinner. She made a lasagna big enough to feed an army and Caden said if we don't get our asses over there soon, he wouldn't wait any longer to dive into the homemade Italian bread he's had to smell all afternoon." Connor turned his horse, saying over his shoulder, "You, too, Nan."

Dan gave her a direct, pointed look as he reached down to unlatch the gate. "No use arguing. I know Tamara can clear the fence, but you'd better play it safe with our expectant momma and come through this way."

Nan steered Lady through the gate, wondering at the way Dan switched to his stern Dom voice when he'd said not to argue. Was he just assuring she would join them, or sending her another message she was missing? Yeah, she definitely needed to return to the club and find another partner to aid her in getting back into the swing of things. Ignoring the twinge in her chest at that decision, she followed them to Caden and Sydney's place.

Dan didn't care for the wan, strained fatigue tightening Nan's face, or the suspicious worry that still lingered today over her odd behavior last night. Outwardly, she acted with the same flirty friendliness he enjoyed as much as her sexual submissiveness. But another sudden uncharacteristic urge to go all Dom on her even though they weren't at the club, returned even stronger than at the diner. As they rode toward Caden's sprawling ranch house, all he could think about was hauling her off that mare and demanding answers to the building perplexities surrounding her long, unexplained absence and the changes in her behavior.

"God, I think I can smell that bread out here," Nan groaned as she dismounted at the barn and tethered Lady to the rail.

"Let's hope there's some left." Connor snatched Tamara's hand as soon as she secured Galahad. "Come on. I'm starving."

Dan slung his arm around Nan's shoulders, a casual gesture he'd done a thousand times over the last few years. But, instead of leaning against him with the natural ease he was used to, she walked alongside him with a wary stiffness that cut him to the quick. Frowning, he nudged his hat back and gazed down at her as they crossed the wide green lawn separating the house from the barns.

"I do something to piss you off, hon?" he asked bluntly.

"What?" Her startled eyes swung up and then away before he could read anything behind the look. "No, of course not. It's just been more tiring getting my shop back open, and the apartment aired out than I expected. I'm worn out."

"Maybe you're trying to do too much too fast." *And maybe there's something you're not telling anyone.* He didn't like that possibility. "You never could take things slow." Testing her, he tightened his arm and added, "Except when you're naked and restrained. You always like things to go slow then."

She didn't rise to the bait, not like she would have before her trip, with teasing, sex-laced innuendos. "It's been awhile, so I guess I'll have to see if that's still true." Pulling away from him as they reached the wraparound porch, she kept her face averted as Connor held open the door with a look of curiosity toward Dan.

Shrugging, Dan said under his breath, "Don't ask me. I don't have a clue what's going on with her."

Dan's stomach rumbled, revealing his appreciation of the enticing aromas greeting them as soon as they entered the house, but as they congregated around the large dining table, it bothered him when Nan took a seat on the opposite side instead of next to him. Whenever they'd socialized with these friends, and others before, they'd always been comfortable pairing up. Every time she exhibited another inconsistency in behavior from the woman he used to know, he grew more suspicious about what happened during her time away.

"So, is this a special occasion?" Nan asked, scooping a large helping of piping hot lasagna onto her plate before passing the dish to Tamara. "Or is this feast an impromptu meal we happened to be around to be invited to?"

"You were in the right place at the right time, but I say we celebrate your return," Sydney said. "I even baked one of your favorite desserts."

Nan grinned, and Dan was delighted to see the spark in her eyes and that her healthy appetite remained the same. "Boston cream pie? I've always preferred our wine and pizza on girl's night out, but cake rules every time, and this lasagna is great. Damn, girlfriend, you can cook."

"True." Tamara bit into a slice of buttery bread, moaning as she chewed. "I don't care why we're here so long as I can have more of that bread. You've outdone yourself, Sydney."

Glancing at Caden and Connor, Dan noticed the brothers

enjoyed listening to the girls banter back and forth as much as he. He knew Nan and Tamara's friendship went back to their early teens, and that they'd welcomed both Sydney and Avery without reservation, much like everyone did him when he'd chosen to open a practice in Willow Springs. He could never regret settling on the small spread and practicing law part-time so he could also work the ranch. The physical labor helped ease the often boring and occasional frustration of litigation. He did a lot of contract work for businesses and ranchers, as well as the standard bread and butter paperwork of drawing up wills and estate planning. Representing military personnel kept his negotiating skills honed. It was never easy pleading for an early release in front of the brass.

By the time they finished the dessert and were stepping back outside, the lowered sun had painted the eastern horizon a scarlet-streaked amber glow. As they mounted their horses, Dan turned to Nan, admiring the ease with which she swung her long, slender legs over the saddle and the enticing view of her ass in snug denim. He relished many fond memories of her draped across his lap, her bare butt his to do with as he pleased. The way she would embrace each swat, lift and beg for more until she writhed against his thighs in orgasm made those scenes both memorable and special. His hand itched to connect with those soft, plump cheeks again, his need to see and hear her moans of pain induced pleasure getting stronger with each guarded look he caught on her face whenever she glanced his way.

"Did you drive to the Barton's or did Tamara pick you up?" he asked her before the two of them took off.

"I drove. Why?"

"I was going to offer to give you a lift back to your apartment from my place after showing you our new foal." Fuck but he hated the way she kept averting her face whenever he suggested something that involved getting close with him.

"Thanks, but I need to get back. Can I take a rain check?"

He saw the moment she realized that was the second time she asked him for a rain check, something he wasn't above reminding her of regardless of Connor and Tamara standing right there with them. "Sure. I'll add it to the one I gave you last night. Now you owe me a visit to my ranch and a scene at The Barn." He turned and spoke to Connor before she could say anything. "I'll get those sale contracts written up tomorrow and out to you by lunch. Will that work?"

"Yeah, that'll be perfect. Greg and Devin won't be out until mid-afternoon. See you then. I'll come pick you up, Tam," Connor told her. Even though she'd moved into Connor's house a few miles from his brother's, Dan knew she still stabled her horses at her place.

"We'll be back there in about fifteen minutes. Come on, Nan. I'll race you."

Without glancing at Dan or acknowledging his last statement, Nan pulled on Lady's reins and took off after her friend with a wave back. Connor shook his head, a rueful grin tugging at his lips. "My girl loves to race, and win, even if she has to cheat to do so." Looking at Dan, he grew serious. "Our Nan just isn't herself, is she?"

"No," Dan agreed as they set out. "I wish she'd tell us, or the girls what really went down in New Orleans."

"You could always call her brother and ask him," Connor suggested.

He shook his head, not ready to go behind her back just yet. "Let's give her time. Could be a personal matter that's none of our business and not worth alienating her friendship by prying into it."

"You don't think so, though."

"No," Dan sighed, "I don't think so."

Twenty minutes later, Dan trotted Tank into his stable just as the sky turned pearl gray. The Appaloosa whinnied, happy to be home because that meant a fresh scoop of oats to snack on as he rubbed him down. Hopping off the stallion that had been his first livestock purchase for the ranch, he loosened the underbelly saddle strap, eager himself to turn in. He slid the saddle off and was reaching for the brush as the back door opened and Pete, one of his new hires and the most troubled, walked in.

"What's up, Sergeant?" The thirty-year-old vet had been rising up the ranks at a steady pace until he'd witnessed half his platoon's deaths in a surprise attack while stationed in Afghanistan. Not even drugs could dull his nightmares, as he'd discovered when they led to his incarceration. His lined face and haunted eyes revealed the toll of what he'd lived through and the ravages of his addiction.

"I saw you come in. Need any help?" Pete walked over, stroked the young filly's nose with a fond smile then picked up another brush and started grooming Tank on the other side of Dan.

"Thanks. Tank here will be in hog heaven with the dual attention, but you're off the clock. Wouldn't you rather be relaxing?" He felt he had to ask, even though Dan knew the younger, troubled man preferred keeping busy right up until exhaustion forced him to his bed in the small bunkhouse he shared with Morales and his foreman, Bernie. His other two hands drove over each day from Billings.

"Nah, I'm good, boss. Besides, Bernie and Morales are going on hour two of a chess game and I can only stand to sit and watch them or TV for so long. The little one is gettin' prettier every day, isn't she?"

Pete's wistful tone tugged at Dan, as did the way his hands weren't quite steady as he brushed along Tank's white and dark brown speckled flanks. He'd been working on the ranch now for six months, and in that time, Dan had caught him smoking pot twice. The lapses had come early after his release, as he'd still been acclimating to civilian life and freedom. Only one hired parolee had tested Dan's three strikes and you're out rule when

Stan had jumped right back into cocaine use within a month of his release. He was hoping Pete wouldn't be his second failure as he was fond of the guy who didn't care for people but held a soft spot for all animals, including the wildlife that came wandering around.

"Yeah, she is. What did you do with the orphaned rabbits?" Pete found the small nest behind the barn yesterday, and what remained of the mother a few yards away.

"Bernie gave me some old lumber and helped me build a safe pen for them. As soon as they get bigger, I'll turn them loose." A rare smile creased his lean cheeks. "Caught Morales trying to hand feed them some lettuce. You should have seen how red he got."

Dan's other new hand was a big, tough ex-marine who talked and laughed loud and hated being alone, Pete's exact opposite and yet the two had hit it off from the start. "Next time, get a picture." Setting aside the brush, he opened Tank's stall and filled the feeder with oats. "Thanks for your help. I've got paperwork to do this evening. You going to be okay?" he asked, confident Pete knew exactly what he wanted to know.

"Yeah, I'm good, boss. I promise. Sometimes…" He hesitated and looked away. "Sometimes it's hard to close my eyes when I know what I'll see. It helps if I can wait until I'm too tired to dream, ya know?"

"I hear you." Shutting the stall gate, he slapped Pete on the back. "You've got me now, though, and Bernie. Do you want to set up an early appointment with Dr. Sorensen?" One of his requirements for giving these guys a job and a second chance was they had to agree to regular sessions with the psychologist in Billings, who also happened to be a veteran and a good friend of Dan's.

"Already did for tomorrow afternoon. I guess I'll go see if those two are still at it. Thanks, boss."

"Goodnight, Pete."

Nan brushed her clammy hands down the silky, thigh-skimming cream sheath she'd chosen to wear to the club tonight. Friday rolled around way too fast for her peace of mind, the busy days and the fun of catching up with patrons and friends doing little to calm the jitters every time she thought of allowing someone to restrain her again. Then there was the nausea she experienced whenever she tried to conjure up the excitement she used to feel at turning herself over to a Dom's complete control. Standing in indecision, looking into her mirror, she wondered if she should wait and put off going again until tomorrow night. She hadn't been this nervous last week, her first time back. But then, that was before experiencing that humiliating flashback, and the uncertainty and trepidation it stirred up.

A surge of anger forced her shoulders back, the move thrusting her braless breasts out and shifting the soft material over her nipples. "Fuck that." Fisting her hands on her hips, she stomped one bare foot and glared at herself. "Get a grip and get over it already. I. Will. Not. Let that bastard win." There. She nodded, feeling a touch more confident after repeating the line she'd first heard from Jay. Damn, she missed her brother, the way he knew when she needed pampering and when it was time to give her a stern, rebuking lecture. He was a lot like Master Dan that way.

Nope, not going there. As much as she cared for Dan, and maybe because she did, she wouldn't seek him out tonight. She wanted over this hurdle, needed to get herself back to where she was before she made that monumental mistake in New Orleans, and she wanted to get there without revealing that mistake to anyone. She wouldn't be able to accomplish that goal if she submitted to her favorite Master tonight. Her shoulders slumped as she contemplated how she could pull that off considering the two thin white scars marring her smooth back, physical proof of the abuse Gerard had heaped upon her.

Turning away from the mirror, she snatched up a light, summer cover, slipped on her sandals and padded to the door before she talked herself out of going. Depending on the apparatus she, or the Dom she hooked up with selected, she would either leave the thin dress on or strip. Back facing him, on; back hidden, off. A simple solution, she told herself as she flipped on both the kitchen and living area lights before locking the door behind her.

Chapter 5

The same pulsating energy that greeted Nan last week sent a thrill through her as she entered the playroom of The Barn. She was early, as the small gathering attested to, but that worked in her favor, at least this time around. There was a time when she'd basked in the pleasure of baring herself in front of a large crowd, confident and unabashed in her nudity. She ached to do so again, craved that freedom with every fiber of her being. As she padded across the gleaming, hardwood floor and a few appreciative male eyes landed on her swaying, unfettered breasts, she experienced a familiar ripple of pleasure, which helped boost her self-esteem as she slid onto a bar stool next to Avery.

"Hi. Did I beat Sydney and Tamara tonight?"

Avery smiled. "Hey, Nan. Yeah, but they'll be here soon. Sorry I didn't make it for our weekly afternoon tea. I got tied up in Billings at the office."

"You're working too much," Grayson insisted as he strode over from behind the bar. "Between the diner and your IT work, you're wearing yourself out, and I don't like it."

Avery sighed. "I told you, Grayson... *ouch!*" She reached up and rubbed her chin where her husband pinched her. "*Master* Grayson," she grumbled with a glare when he lifted a brow and waited for her correction. "With the extra tourism Willow Springs has been getting from the new dude ranch, Gertie needs my help. I'll cut back when things slow down."

"She should hire extra help," Nan put in. "I've been swamped also, but my menu is small, and easy compared to hers. But I have to admit, I don't mind profiting from Greg and Devin's business."

The two men they were discussing entered just then, their striking dual presence drawing more eyes than hers. Tall and muscled, the ex-FBI agents exuded enough dominance in just their riveted gazes and confident strides to dampen the panties of any sub who was lucky enough to catch their interest. Like every other man in ranch country, they wore snug denim and boots and Nan guessed they'd left their Stetsons in the foyer closet. Even Dan wore jeans and boots daily, only when he was in lawyer mode, he dressed them up with a casual sport coat.

No, not going there! She needed to be thinking about and considering any Dom to hook up with other than the one who could read her every move and decipher every expression. Or, in Masters Greg and Devin's case, two men. They had been new members before she left, and she didn't know them well since she'd only enjoyed one scene with the duo that did not include sex. It had been her first and only ménage, and as they headed toward the bar, a stirring of expectation rippled down her spine, sending a wave of relief through her.

"Why are you glaring at us, Sheriff?" Devin asked, cocking his head as he stood next to Nan's stool. The tight stretch of his black tee shirt emphasized the thick bulge of his shoulders and upper arms and the dark blue of his midnight eyes.

"I'm blaming you two for my wife's harried schedule. Gertie's got her working extra hours due to the visitors you keep sending to town."

Greg laughed, his moss green eyes twinkling as he held up both hands, as if to ward him off. "Hey, don't shoot at the hands that are feeding you. It's not our fault we're as good at running a new business as we are at making the subs here happy." His bright gaze swiveled toward Nan as he shifted behind her stool. "Speaking of which, it's good to see you again, Nan. We didn't get a chance to welcome you back last week."

At the reminder of her hasty exit, she looked away from both his and Devin's scrutinizing looks. The way the two of them closed her in by standing so close, leaving her no way to move out of their reach unless she shoved one of them or Avery aside, sent a frisson of unease skating under her skin. Refusing to give in to it, she forced a confident smile as she turned to face them again.

"It's great to be back. I've missed everyone. I've heard praises for your dude ranch all week. Congratulations."

"Thank you."

Devin squeezed her shoulder, the heat of his palm and strength of his grip warming her, as did the way his midnight eyes lowered to her breasts. Why the hell couldn't her head get on board with her body?

"What can I get everyone?" Grayson asked before telling Avery, "Hold off on your second drink, sugar. I have plans for you as soon as Connor arrives and takes over here."

Avery flushed, but her nipples went to turgid pinpoints under her satin tee and a spark of excitement lit her eyes behind the dark frames. "Yes, Sir," she returned without hesitation.

"I'll have a light beer." Nan stuck with a milder brew rather than going with hard liquor as that tended to hit her much harder and faster. She needed a nerve boost before taking advantage of the interest Masters Devin and Greg were exhibiting, but nothing that would dull her senses. Between the way the close confines of their bodies rattled her and her body's happy response to Greg's simple touch, she would need all her wits about her to go through with a scene with the two of them, even if it was mild compared to what she was used to.

"We need a girl's night," Avery told Nan as the guys started talking about plans to expand the dude ranch already.

Clasping the cold bottle, Nan took a long drink before replying, "I'm in whenever you can get the time. All of my evenings are free but I don't know about Sydney and Tamara. Speaking of getting together, Alice posted a flyer on a book fair this Sunday. Can you get away long enough to check it out with me?"

"I'll make time," Avery answered with a nod.

They talked books while she sipped her beer, the conversation distracting her from the two men's crowding until Devin trailed his calloused fingers over her arm as Greg cupped her shoulders and drew her back against him. Gulping down the last swallow, she relished the small spark of arousal their dual touch ignited. It offered her a surge of hope and confidence as Devin dipped his head and whispered in her ear.

"Care to join us upstairs?"

A shudder of longing coursed through her, boosting the hum of arousal enough to defy the fraction of doubt still clouding her head. Calling on her steadfast determination to get her life back, she ignored the nervous flutters in her stomach and accepted their invitation. "Why yes, Sir, I would like that."

His low chuckle reverberated down her spine. "Excellent."

In a coordinated move that smacked of experience, they each clasped a hand and drew her to her feet, keeping her between them with snug grips. "Excuse us," Greg told Grayson and Avery.

"Catch you later, Avery," Nan tossed back as the two men wasted no time prodding her toward the stairs. *I've gone up these stairs countless times,* she lectured herself as her heartbeat picked up speed with each step up she took. The heat of their bodies in front and behind her helped keep the ever-present coldness pushed to the back burner as they reached the loft and the telltale sounds of BDSM play taking place resonated around the upper level.

Good memories of being bound on the St. Andrew Cross Sue Ellen now occupied popped into her head as they walked past several other apparatus already in use. Despite the dimmer lighting upstairs, she could still see the pink stripes adorning Leslie's perspiration-slick breasts and thighs and the glow shining on her face from her bound position on the wooden A-frame. The pleasure she reaped from the switch her Dom was applying was obvious from her writhing acceptance and glistening labia.

It was so easy for Nan to remember the pain induced heightened arousal she once embraced from the switch as well as other implements, but as Devin and Greg halted at a chain station and reached for the narrow straps of her sheath, panic clawed its way into her throat. She couldn't risk exposing her scars, not yet. She had hurdles to overcome before that could happen.

"No," she croaked, startling both Doms. "I mean, I'd rather leave it on for now. I'm sorry. It's…" Floundering for an excuse, she settled on a partial truth. "It's been awhile."

Master Greg raised a skeptical brow but nodded along with his partner. Lifting her arms up to the dangling cuffs, he surprised her with his memory of the one time they scened together over a year ago. "Do you still use panda as your safeword?"

She nodded, pleased with their recall. The collection of pandas she'd been amassing since childhood made it easy to remember. "Yes, I do."

"And are you good with me removing this?" Devin slid a hand under her short dress and snapped the thin strap of her thong against her hip.

That small pain ricocheted down to her pussy, causing Nan to jerk her pelvis forward in an automatic response of acceptance that drew her smile. "Yes, Sir, that can go." She was pleased with her progress as he stripped the underwear down her legs and she kicked them aside but froze in immediate indecision as they bent to restrain her ankles two feet apart on a spreader bar, the move triggering an unwanted memory.

Nan whimpered as she struggled against the ropes binding her ankles and wrists so tightly together she could no longer feel them, only smell the trickle of blood oozing from the cuts into her skin. "Cry out all you want," Master Gerard stated with calm smugness before locking her in the pitch-black room in his cellar. "This room is soundproof; no one will hear. You can think about your defiance until I return." The slam of the door and a key turning scared her more than anything else he'd done.

Hard hands cupped her face as other hands stroked up her legs. "Nan, open your eyes and look at me," Devin demanded in a tone not to be ignored as he held her head immobile, refusing to let her turn away.

Blinking her eyes open, Nan returned to the present and her current surroundings. Taking a deep, shuddering breath, she forced a crooked smile while praying for a return of the pleasant sensations she'd been starting to feel.

"Sorry, but I want to pass on the ankle restraints. Like I said, it's been awhile." She didn't dare look away from their concerned, probing stares, but held her breath until they nodded.

Greg slid one hand up her inner thigh, pausing with a tight grip an inch away from the bare flesh of her labia. "Is there anything else we need to know?"

Their implacable holds brought a return of the heat she craved; their calm patience gave her the courage she needed to continue. "No, Sirs, I'm good now." She teased them with a flirty grin, saying, "Please, continue."

Nan couldn't decipher the look they exchanged but as Devin inched around behind her and Greg shifted his hand to press up between her legs, she decided she didn't care what they were thinking. Closing her eyes, the darkness brought up the face of a different Dom other than the two giving her their undivided attention. She didn't want to think about a pair of dark brown eyes and a rugged, tanned face emphasized by sun-streaked, sandy blond hair when her body was stirring to life under the four hands and two mouths of two other men. *Damn it, Master Dan, you weren't there when I needed you, and I don't need you now.*

Opening her eyes, she forced away both his image and the unfair thought it pulled from her subconscious as hard hands pushed up her dress and cupped her buttocks. Devin squeezed her butt as he leaned around and whispered in her ear, "Just as soft and malleable as I remember."

"The same here," Greg said, exploring the flesh of her plump folds with his calloused fingertips as he brushed his lips over hers.

A welcome rush of heated dampness filled her pussy and Nan moaned from the surprising return of the pleasure she'd been seeking. As they continued to fondle her, dipping their fingers between her cheeks and slit, she found herself wishing for the added stimulus of hot, throbbing pain, biting her lip when the bad memories of excruciating agony wanted to return.

"Please," she whispered, forcing herself to keep her eyes open as she rocked her hips forward and back, desperate now for them to move faster before the past could come back to ruin everything.

"In a hurry?" Devin smacked her ass, the sting a startling pleasure. "I suppose, if it's been that long, we can accommodate you, can't we, Master Greg?"

"I can make a concession this one time." He thrust up inside her, skimming her clit and bringing her to her toes.

Nan basked in the goosebumps popping up as tingles of plea-sure tickled her spasming pussy. Shifting her eyes away from Master Greg's continued, intent observation of her every expres-sion, she took in the scenes going on near them, enjoying the voyeurism as much as the arousal she'd achieved after the long dry spell. With her concentration centered on the teasing strokes between her buttocks skimming the sensitive rim of her anus and the deeper, faster thrusts teasing the swelling tissues of her vagina and her eyes focused on others, she jolted, unprepared for the slash of sudden pain as a flogger struck her ass for the first time in over a year.

She cried out, struggling with a chaotic mix of emotions as another swat sent blistering streaks of heated pain across her buttocks. Desperate to keep the encroaching fear from reaching the forefront, she tried recalling the times when she'd embraced the prickling hurt, relished every strike of the leather strands and the ecstasy she'd reaped from them. Writhing in her bonds, she fought against the past and everything Master Gerard subjected her to in such a short time, but the darkness encroached anyway, and with it a cold shiver of fearful memories.

"You dare to tell me no with a fucking safeword?" Gerard yanked her off the spanking bench and dragged her toward the basement stairs.

Nan's irritation changed to instant terror as he ignored her demands to let her go and hauled her down to a damp, dark cellar. Shoving her to the concrete floor, she winced as her hip exploded in pain. But that was nothing compared to the fiery lash streaking across her back as he struck her with a single-tailed whip she never saw him pick up. The shock and pain rendered her speechless long enough for him to strike her again.

"You'll learn your place soon enough. No cunt refuses me."

"You fucking bastard!" she screamed as her skin split with the third lash. She tried to stand, but he kicked her back down, robbing her of breath as her rib cracked with the impact of his booted foot. With panic clawing its way into her throat, she crawled naked across the floor, seeking relief from the excruciating agony exploding across her back. The metallic smell of her own blood followed her, as did he, until she reached a corner and curled into a ball of petrified physical and mental torment.

Nan's harsh breathing turned to whimpering sobs and she slammed her eyes shut against the mortification of failure, never seeing the third man rushing to her side or feeling his soothing hands reaching for her. But it was Master Dan's insistent, deep voice that penetrated the haze of terror gripping her, his tall, hard body she fell against as her hands were freed. Shaking, her body broken out in a cold sweat, she ignored the worried questions firing from Greg and Devin and clung to the steady beat of Master Dan's heart under her ear, his voice whispering in her ear.

Dan tried to control his raging emotions as he held onto Nan's quivering body. The displeasure he'd felt upon coming up to the loft and spotting her with his two friends had surprised him. Both Greg and Devin held reputations as excellent Doms, and he would trust any sub with them, so his quick reaction to seeing their hands all over her was odd and would need further examining later. As he took up his responsibility as monitor and settled against the back wall to keep an eye on things, he couldn't help sliding his gaze back over to the threesome every few minutes, and what he kept seeing sent up a red flag of warning and unease.

He knew from personal experience how much his favorite sub enjoyed sexual submission, and how a long session over his lap or with his flogger would send her into orgasmic orbit. So, why was she tensing when Devin spanked her ass, and why did her jaw tighten and her face turn sheet-white when he switched to the flogger? Other than the gyrations of her body signaling her acceptance and growing arousal from their attentions, he saw none of her familiar signs of an impending orgasm. Even those telltale body movements ceased after just a few short moments, fear and gut-wrenching cries taking their place.

"Breathe, hon. I've got you," he murmured in her ear, the seed of suspicion her odd behavior since returning had planted blossomed into a full bloom of certainty as he held her. Something happened that had stolen her confidence and pleasure in the lifestyle she loved, the possibilities of what stirring his anger into a feverish pitch.

"Fuck, Dan, what the hell is going on?" Devin ground out, his look as confused, concerned and pissed off as Greg's. "She never spoke her safeword, or even red. We didn't catch on until you did."

"I don't know but intend to find out." Nan stiffened, and he guessed she was coherent enough to catch what they were saying.

Before he could ease her back, she pushed against him and demanded in a low voice, "Let me go."

He dropped his arms, not wanting to traumatize her further. As she stepped back and averted her ravaged face, his chest tightened and his abdomen cramped from the surge of frustration and fury over what might have befallen her in New Orleans.

"Nan..."

She held up a hand that still shook and turned to face Devin and Greg. "I apologize, Sirs. I don't know what came over me. I'm tired, but that's no excuse. Maybe I'm just not ready to jump back into things after so long away."

Since she refused direct eye contact with them and kept her back to Dan, she didn't see the disbelief on all three of their faces. Dan clenched his hands into fists to keep from spinning her around and demanding the truth. Going all caveman on her sure as hell wasn't the way to handle this woman, or the situation he never dreamed she would end up in.

As Greg handed her her discarded panties, Dan said, "In that case, I'll walk you out." She whipped around, gripping the silky thong, her gold eyes sparking with irritation. At least the glazed look of terror had cleared. Before she could turn him down, he insisted, not hesitating to exert his control over this matter. "Yes, I will, and you'll either comply or I'll file a complaint and request the suspension of your club privileges." He was counting on the desire he'd seen in her actions and on her face for getting back what she'd apparently lost while away to gain her compliance.

"Fine," she bit out, not bothering to hide her displeasure with his threat. Stepping into the thong, she yanked it up with no sign of embarrassment before heading toward the stairs.

"You find out anything, we'd appreciate you filling us in," Greg said as Dan started after Nan.

Lifting his hand in acknowledgement, he nodded, saying, "Will do," and went after his girl. He caught up with her at the top of the stairs and snatched her hand. "Damn it, Nan. I'm just trying to help." Stepping in front of her, he trotted down the stairs, tugging her behind him.

"I don't need your help, or anyone else's," she hissed.

"You couldn't prove that ten minutes ago," Dan shot back, ignoring the curious looks aimed their way as he strode toward the foyer, keeping a tight grip on her hand, her damp palm and quivering fingers proof she remained shaken. He was forced to release her so she could get her shoes and cover, but instead of arguing further, she remained mulishly silent.

He followed her out to her car but as she reached for the handle, he spun her to face him with a gentle grip on her shoulders. "Damn it, Nan, what the fuck happened to you?" he snapped with concerned exasperation.

Her face tightened with mortified frustration before she returned in an angry whisper, "What happened was I trusted the wrong person, was dumb enough to believe the wrong Dom. It was my mistake, and I'm working through it, and that's all you need to know. Now, back off."

Dan dropped his hands and stepped back far enough to reach around her and open the door. She slid behind the wheel and reached for the handle, but he kept her from closing it as he leaned down and said, "You're wrong. That's not all I need to know and you're not working through it, but around it. We'll talk more about this later, when we've both cooled down. Try to get some rest."

Nan gripped the steering wheel and clenched her teeth as she drove back to her apartment with unfulfilled arousal warring with a past that kept playing head games with her. By the time she entered her well-lit apartment, she didn't know who she was more upset and angry with—Gerard for not being the strict but caring Dom she'd been seeking, herself for her failure to get over and move on from what he'd put her through, or Dan, who insisted she let him past her guard. Tossing her purse onto the dainty table just inside the door, she stomped her foot and shook her head in a fit of exasperation. Damn it, she knew it wasn't fair to blame Dan for being not only a good Dom, but a caring friend.

She kicked off her sandals and padded toward her bedroom, stripping the slip of a dress off over her head as she recalled the clutch around her heart when his rough voice penetrated her fear and she knew he would catch her as her hands were released. Of all the men she'd submitted to, he was the only one she'd ever given her complete trust and submission to. But considering her lapse tonight, could she even count on old feelings, confidences and friends to get her over this hurdle when the arousing attentions of two men had failed?

Falling into bed, she hugged her largest stuffed panda to her, a gift from Jay, despairing of ever freeing herself of Gerard's brutality.

The next day was busier than usual for a Saturday due to the arts and crafts fair taking place in the town square that went along with the book fair at the library she had made plans to attend with Avery tomorrow. Nan enjoyed her regulars as much as the visitors coming into Willow Springs to shop at the booths of handcrafted goods, but despite being run ragged with orders and sales, her mind remained preoccupied with the decision on whether to return to The Barn tonight. Her friends expected her, and likely Master Dan did too. But every time she tried to imagine herself in another scene, being bound to one of her favorite apparatus, she broke out in a cold sweat. It wasn't the return of the painful bad memories that caused the nauseous churning in her stomach, but the fear of failing again, of letting down those friends and another Dom.

Ignoring a text invite from Tamara to join her, Sydney, Avery and their spouses at the diner before going to the club, she waved goodbye to the last customer to leave and started to lock the shop's front door when Willa from the library popped in. Holding a foil-wrapped plate, the elderly woman handed it to her with a smile.

"I'm glad I caught you. Alice and I saved these aside for you this morning when she arrived at my place early to help me bake for the bake sale. I hope brownies are still your favorite."

"You bet." Touched, Nan came around the counter, took the plate and gave Willa a hug in appreciation for her thoughtfulness. "Thank you so much, and tell Alice thank you. I'll be over tomorrow as soon as I close at four and return your plate."

"Wonderful. We have a good selection of new titles you'll like. See you then."

Nan locked the door behind her and closed the blinds before turning to clean up, which gave her another hour to wrestle with her indecision about going out tonight. By the time she shut off the lights and trudged upstairs, she was dragging her feet with both mental and physical exhaustion, carrying the plate of brownies.

"Fuck it," she muttered, entering her apartment and closing the door behind her to lean against it with a weary sigh. "And fuck you, *Master* Gerard." The man she'd met at a casual, friendly BDSM mixer could have won an Oscar for his acting skills. The persona of a strict but considerate Dom he portrayed to ingratiate himself into the local club had disappeared as soon as she refused to be his sexual and subservient slave. After their initial meeting at the mixer, her brother Jay left for Houston to assist with a case linked to one of his. During his week-long absence, she'd given in to her boredom and the needs begging to be met since hearing Master Gerard's deep voice and seeing the lustful interest reflected in his pitch-black eyes.

Following a few dates in public places, Nan had played it smart and careful when she'd accepted Gerard's third invitation to dine at his mansion by texting Jay of her plans and location. She hadn't been smart or careful when she let her guard down and fell for the considerate 'we'll take it slow so I can learn what you need from submission' line he fed her to get her to stay at his place until Jay returned instead of heeding the shivers his cold, calculated stares gave her. He'd backed up that line by putting her in the guest bedroom of his two-story, historical home the first night and not making any moves. The second day there, he'd given her a glimpse of his dungeon in the basement, and she'd been torn between fascinated curiosity and the first prickles of alarm gazing at the medieval implements and furniture of torture he'd amassed had produced.

On the third night, he bound her to the bed, his black eyes lacking any warmth or approval as he brought her body to the brink of climax over and over with sharp snaps of a flogger only to stop before she could go over. By the time she curled under the covers, her body throbbing with heated pain front and back and he'd walked out with orders not to touch herself, she was considering leaving first thing in the morning. Too bad she let herself fall for a return of his outwardly charming demeanor as he served her breakfast on the small veranda by the pool. When he ordered her to strip outdoors an hour later, she'd been both eager to please and to get relief from a long night of unfulfilled arousal. That lasted until she knelt upon his instructions and then refused to agree to be his slave when he laid out what he wanted from her.

Shuddering at the memory of what had come next, Nan pushed away from the door, set the brownies on the end table next to the sofa and went to her small stash of liquor under the television. Getting hauled upstairs and locked in the guest bedroom naked and left with no food and only the bathroom sink for water for four days had been the easiest part of the following week as Master Gerard's captive. Knowing she wouldn't be going anywhere tonight, she gripped the full bottle of bourbon and threw herself onto the sofa, pulling a pillow stitched with an adorable panda face to her chest.

Bringing the bottle to her mouth, she took a long drink as she uncovered the brownies and grabbed one to ease the burn with its chocolate, sugary sweetness. "Perfect," she sighed, licking her fingers before picking up the remote and flicking through the Saturday night fare. Shit, how long had it been since she spent a Saturday night alone in front of the television? Swigging another drink, she tried to think of anything except what she was missing out on by her continued cowardice.

Nan was down to just a fourth of the bourbon left, having finished the four brownies when she nodded off into an inebriated slumber. Seconds, minutes or hours later – she didn't know which – abrupt pounding on her door jarred her onto the floor next to where she'd kicked off her jeans. The room spun and nausea churned in her stomach as she stumbled to her feet, her fuzzy brain trying to make sense of someone showing up this late unannounced. The uncomfortable taste of bile inched up to her throat as she lurched toward the door. Peeking through the peep hole with one blurry eye, she gritted her teeth and swore under her breath when she made out Dan's tall form, glimpsing the curl of his blond hair around his nape from under his Stetson.

She didn't think twice about flinging open the door wearing nothing but a tee decorated with a large steaming teacup that skimmed the top of her thighs and barely covered her panties. Hell, she thought, the man had seen, touched and tasted every inch of her naked body countless times. Why that caused her pussy to spasm in warm response as annoyance clouded her already fuzzy head, she didn't know and didn't care.

Glaring up into his tanned, rugged face, she struggled to keep upright by leaning against the door jamb as she grumbled, "Don't know why y're here, don't frickin' care. Go 'way." Slamming the door, she spun around and ran into the back of the couch just as he walked inside, ignoring her dismissal.

"Damn it!" She whirled, and he caught her as her head went on a fast roller coaster ride around the room. "Whoa." She leaned against his wide chest and sighed, mumbling, "Go 'way." again.

Chapter 6

D an held onto Nan, trying to ignore the urge to strip off her top and fill his hands with the lush breasts pressed against his chest. He ached to touch her again almost as much as he needed to find out what she'd been through while away. He'd spent the last few hours at the club, frustrated with her absence but determined to give her more time before confronting her about the truth. That decision had only lasted until he failed to drum up any enthusiasm or interest in choosing a sub to play with, not even to take his mind off the one who had occupied his thoughts the most since first witnessing her eager enthusiasm to please a Dom while embracing her need for painful stimulation. It hurt the way she'd shut him out, as much as it agonized him to see her looking so defiantly despondent as she ordered him to leave.

"Not going to happen, hon. Jesus," he swore as he spotted the near empty liquor bottle. "Please tell me that wasn't full when you started this binge."

She shook her head and pulled back and he got a good look at her pale face. "Can't. Sick."

Letting her go, he shook his head as he followed her awkward dash to the bathroom. He stopped the slam of that door with his hand and refused to give in to her cursing insistence for him to leave as she fell to her knees in front of the commode. As she threw up, he wetted a washcloth in cold water then leaned over and wiped her perspiring, flushed face while flushing the toilet.

"Is that it for now?"

"I'm not talking tonight, so go 'way." She made a feeble attempt to push him away.

"Baby, you're going to have to come up with something else to say or keep quiet. Come on, up you go." Dan led her out of the bathroom with an arm around her shoulders and back into the living room to grab her jeans. "I'm parked out back, so we can just carry these with us. Let's go."

Nan stiffened and braced her feet, halting their trek to the door and drawing his eyes to her long, slender legs. Fuck, but he really liked those legs. "Where?" she asked with a suspicious glare that curtailed the quick spurt of lust.

"My place. I'm not leaving you alone like this and I have to be up early. And don't worry, I have no intention of betraying your trust by taking advantage of your state to pry answers out of you. You will be stone-cold sober when you tell me what happened." She opened her mouth to argue and anger overrode his concern. "Don't fucking argue with me, Nan. I'm already a hair's breadth away from sending my good intentions to Hell by hauling you across my lap and spanking answers from you." Knowing him as well as she did, she must have seen how serious, and how frustrated he was because she nodded despite her own annoyance flaring in her red-rimmed eyes.

Luck was with him when she fell asleep on the ride out to his house, which made it easy for him to scoop her up and carry her into the guest room she was no stranger to. After tucking her in, he locked up, tugged off his boots and shirt and settled in the wide cushioned chair next to the bed. He preferred ensuring she would sleep well now rather than being roused from his bed right after getting into it when he got up early to do chores.

Some indefinable emotion rolled through him as he watched her restless shifts and listened to her mumble. He remembered how much he'd missed her while she was away, how he'd taken it personally when she stopped answering his texts and calls even though she'd done the same with her girlfriends. He'd been itching to put his hands on her soft flesh again ever since she returned, craving to hear that breathy catch in her throat as he striped her skin red with a reed-thin cane or leather strap and ached to sink into her tight, wet heat. She was the one woman he never tired of dominating and the only one he'd allowed himself to develop a close, fond friendship with.

Which made it even more difficult to remain calm as she cried out in sudden terror, her slim body twitching as if in pain that went beyond what she'd always reaped pleasure from. She settled down as he leaned forward and brushed his fingers down her clammy cheek, whispering, "Shh, Nan, I'm right here." He jerked as if struck when she responded with a whimper and pleaded in a tone and with words that cut him to the quick.

"Help me, Dan, Master... please, help..."

Nan drifted into a deeper sleep on a soft moan, leaving him sitting there struggling to contain the rage her fearful pleadings had unleashed. Unwarranted guilt took a painful swat at Dan, adding to the escalating, pounding pressure to punish whoever had hurt her. Not trusting himself, or the unaccustomed emotions her traumatized state unearthed, he surged to his feet and left her sleeping quietly. With fury burning like acid in his gut, he knew sleep was out of the question. With her quivering voice calling for him echoing in his head, he stormed out to the barn. He never felt the soft grass beneath his bare feet, or the concrete floor of the small horse stable, or the straw scattered around the hanging punch bag in the farthest corner.

Foregoing the padded boxing gloves hanging on the wall, he

pulled back his bare fists and proceeded to pummel the inanimate object with all the pent-up fury raging inside him. Possible scenarios ran through his mind as his muscles strained, his breathing turned harsh and the tight skin covering his knuckles split. He was so mired in his tormented thoughts, he didn't hear Bernie enter through the side door until the older man who'd quickly become more of a father figure to him than the one he'd never known reached out and stopped the swaying of the bag.

Bernie's shrewd hazel eyes took in Dan's sweaty face and bare, heaving chest with a lifted brow before he asked, "Something bothering you, boy?"

"Shit." Dan blew out a breath as he bent at the waist, bracing his hands on his thighs and noticing for the first time his bleeding knuckles. "Yeah, Bernie, you could say that." Before he could ask what, Dan said, "But I don't have any answers for either of us."

Straightening, it didn't surprise him to see Bernie handing him the tube of Campho-Phenique he was never without. "Thanks." Taking it, he relished the burning sting of the medicine as he dabbed the cream on his cuts. "I have a guest tonight, Nan, who went through something bad. That's all I know."

Cocking his graying head, the shorter man returned, "But you'll find out."

Handing him back the ointment, he said with unequivocal surety, "Damn right."

"Then I'll say goodnight and see you in the morning. Try to get some sleep."

Dan caught his breath as he watched Bernie exit as quietly as he'd entered, the soft spot he held for his right-hand man turning even mushier. With a sigh of disgust aimed at his temporary lapse of control, he swiveled and padded over to the young foal's stall to stroke his fingers down the white star on her head. Compared to the massive spread in northern Montana where he'd grown up as the son of the owner's live-in housekeeper and nanny, his place was nothing more than a blip. But the smaller acreage and herd suited him just fine and gave him the opportunity to work the ranch and keep up with his legal skills. Before hiring Bernie, his single mother had been the only one proud of him for all he'd accomplished.

Now, with having reached forty, he could say he was happy with his choices in life and content with the path he'd chosen going forward. That was, until Nan had returned with haunted eyes that flashed with fear when they should have been glazed with passion and shattered his control with heartbroken pleas for his help when he'd been oblivious to her need. With the aches he incurred starting to make themselves known, he returned to the house hoping for a few hours of sleep before starting the battle for answers in the morning.

Nan rolled over with a groan, her pounding head and dry mouth reminding her of how she'd spent the night before wallowing in self-pity. Disgusted with herself, she sat up and sucked in a deep breath until the room stopped spinning. By the time she oriented herself, she realized she wasn't in her room, but Dan's guest room. She took a moment to search through her limited memory of the previous night and didn't like the vague hints she was getting. Had she really barfed over the toilet as he'd held her hair back and then washed her face? *Geez*, how mortifying. Dropping her aching head into her hands, she dug her fingers into her scalp, despairing of the woman she'd let herself become and of the constant failures to gain control of her life.

Lifting her head, she checked the time on the bedside clock, relieved she still had several hours before she opened the shop at one. Then she spotted the tall glass of orange juice, two white pills next to it and the propped-up note written in Dan's distinctive scrawl. *Take the aspirin and a hot shower — you'll feel better. There's toast in the oven, lightly buttered. Join me in the stable when you're ready.*

That was so like him, she thought as she downed the pain killers and drank the whole glass of juice. He always thought ahead and always knew what she needed. It wasn't the first time she'd ended up in his guest room after a drinking binge. *But never in his bed.* Whoa, where the hell did that thought come from? They didn't have that kind of relationship. It had always been easy for them to maintain a casual friendship when not at the club, and just as easy to slip into a Dom/sub role when inside those walls. Neither of them had ever questioned why that was or wanted anything more.

Sliding out of bed, Nan picked up her jeans off the chair and padded into the attached bathroom. Thirty minutes later, she felt better as she slipped on her sandals, helped herself to the toast and strolled outside wondering what she would say to Dan, how much she should tell him now that he'd seen just how traumatized she'd been. The submissive side of her knew she could trust him, but the independent part of her nature kept insisting she could and should get over her ordeal with no more help. Jay and doctors had been there when she'd required physical healing. A few visits from a psychologist while still in the hospital were enough to convince her she didn't need or want a shrink poking into her head.

Nibbling the toast, she entered the stable and took an appreciative whiff of hay and horses, smells only someone who loved animals could appreciate. Scanning the stalls, she spotted Dan inside the last one, his hat shielding his expression as he ran a brush over the silky coat of a black and white spotted Appaloosa filly. The foal's small head rubbed against him in affection and Nan's heart turned over at the sight.

As she stepped toward them, her mouth went dry looking at the gentle way he stroked the young horse, and then watered as she took in the dark blue tee shirt stretched over his wide shoulders, emphasizing his thick biceps. As usual, his long legs were encased in tight denim, his boots showing the wear and tear of years and outdoor work. Even though she was five foot eight, his towering height forced her head to crane back as she entered the stall and looked up at him.

Glancing at her from the other side of the foal, Dan nudged his hat back and pinned her with a dark, searching gaze. "Good morning. You look much better," he greeted her with a nod.

Nan tilted her lips in a self-deprecating smile. "I guess a bottle of bourbon and four brownies on an empty stomach isn't a good idea." The lingering abdominal queasiness still felt uncomfortable, but she figured nerves might have more to do with that than the alcohol.

"Probably not, but then, when demons won't leave you alone, what can you do? Oh." He snapped his fingers. "I know. You can come to a friend and tell him what happened, who hurt you."

She sighed, glanced away and then faced him again, squaring her shoulders. "Damn it, Dan, it's not that easy." Reaching out a hand that suddenly shook, she brushed her fingers along the filly's long neck, falling in love with the doe eyes she turned on her. "She's beautiful." Nan got a head rub that made her melt. "And so sweet."

"Did he rape you?"

The abruptness of the question startled her and her eyes flew to his face and his rigid jaw. She blew out a breath as she conceded she owed him for the decent night's sleep last night, even if he had arrived uninvited and unwanted. "No, thank God. He made it painfully clear I had to learn my place before I earned the privilege of his cock."

Those chocolate eyes flashed with outrage on her behalf. "Jesus, Nan, how the hell did you end up with such a bastard? Was he a sadist?" He came around the horse and gripped her shoulders as she made to turn away. "No. No more hiding, no more running. I want to understand, and then I want to help. Tell me."

Longing for what he was offering, and what she craved,

coiled inside her, but the fear of failing again was still there, as was the shame in admitting to her own stupidity. "An hour with a sadist would have been a welcome respite compared to what he did," she admitted in a low, shaky voice before looking up at him and pulling out of his grasp. Masking her expression with calm assurance, she said, "I'm fine, Dan." She conjured up a cheeky grin as she added, "But thanks for tucking me in last night and for the morning after cocktail."

"You're fine, huh? So fine you didn't undress Friday night at the club for the first time since I've known you. Before that ass got hold of you, you loved baring yourself in public." He moved close enough she felt his breath whisper across her face as he whispered, "I *loved* how you would embrace nudity with such unabashed enthusiasm. Why didn't you want Master Greg or Master Devin to see your lush breasts?" His dark eyes swept down to her chest and her nipples beaded under his pointed stare. Her breath snagged as he looked back at her and cupped one large hand between her legs, pressing against her pubis. "Or your pretty pussy? You used to get off on just a few pussy spanks."

Nan heated from head to toe, her body flushing with the rapid flow of blood to her girly parts. This was the heady feeling she'd despaired of ever getting back, the beginning of a gripping ache that would torment her until she exploded in a series of pain driven climaxes. Damn it, then he had to go and ruin the fantasy of believing she could achieve that high again as he stepped away from her and pet the little filly.

"You like her, then she's yours. For a price."

Nan stiffened and went cold as she glared at him in disappointment. "There's a price for everything, isn't there? Even friendship."

He winced then hardened his jaw. "Not normally, no, and you fucking well know that. But then again, these aren't normal circumstances, are they?" he returned coolly.

Well, hell, wasn't that the shitty truth? She shrugged, as if it didn't matter to her about that precious baby when in truth she would give her eye teeth to raise the filly as her own. Master Dan knew just how to play her, and reel her in. "Just out of curiosity, what's your price?"

"Your complete trust. Give yourself to me, and not just at the club this time, and agree to my demands. The first time I get you to climax, she's yours, and our bargain can end."

Oh, wow, I never expected that. His suggestion sent warm tingles dancing down her spine, a temptation she was hard-pressed to turn down. A chance to get back the confidence Gerard had stolen from her and win the foal would be a dream come true. She'd always wanted a horse of her own but had intended to wait until she could buy a few acres to keep it on instead of boarding it. But gazing into those soft, trusting eyes had won her over and there was no going back now. She couldn't help thinking that might have been Dan's plan all along.

"I've never known you to be so manipulative," she said without censure.

"I've never been presented with such a challenge before."

Dan reached behind her and wound her hair around his hand and wrist until his knuckles rested against her nape with the snug hold. She held her breath, waiting for the tug, refusing to panic as the flashback of Gerard's cruel grip and drag on her scalp threatened the fond memory of the tug she used to love. But he just held patiently still, his eyes steady on her face, giving her the option to move and create that yank on her scalp herself or to stay still.

"What are you trying to prove?" she asked when her jitters calmed, confused by this maneuver.

"Nothing. I'm showing you I'm willing to let you set the pace and call the shots here first, until you're more comfortable. When you are, I'll take over and then we'll go to the club."

His offer surprised her, the reason for it renewing her frustration. "But, you'll hate that!" When it came to sex, he was a dominant man, needing to control as much as she craved to be taken over. She didn't want her fears to keep him from enjoying the lifestyle like they were her.

A small smile curled his lips. "Yeah, I will. But you'll need that assurance to get you over the first hurdle." He released her hair and pivoted, walking out of the stall, his next words causing a wet gush to dampen her panties. "You used to love going down on me, and in case I've never mentioned it before, no one can give head as good as you, at least from what I remember. I may need a reminder to be sure. I'll be up at the house when you decide."

The casual way Dan tossed out the suggestion for oral sex and the thread of excitement the idea evoked reminded Nan of why she'd always enjoyed his company. *What do I have to lose?* Her first thought propelled her feet forward, her response making her eager to discover if indulging in that sexual act outside of the club would turn her on as much as when she'd performed it in public. But she halted after taking only two steps, her insecurities rising to the surface. What if she freaked out again, like she had the other night? Who would be more upset if she failed to go through with it, if she managed to suck and stroke his cock into a throbbing erection and a return of terror forced her to back away?

The little filly neighed behind her, the sweet sound pulling her back into the stall to stroke her silky head. *Shit*, was she such a fucked-up mess she would walk away from his offer, from the first light at the end of the dark tunnel she'd failed to emerge from on her own? Before she could decide, the side door opened and a young man she didn't recognize entered, his startled gaze taking in her unexpected presence.

"Hi. I'm a friend of Dan's. Are you one of the new hands around here?" His gaunt face reminded her of other veterans Dan had hired and helped in the past.

"Yes, ma'am. I'm Pete." He came over and held out his hand, his brows dipping as he got a close look at her face. "You okay?"

"I'm fine, a little too much to drink last night is all," she returned with a wry grin at his astuteness as she shook his hand. "I'm Nan, and I hope I'm way too young for you to continue calling me ma'am."

A sheepish look crossed his face. "Respectful politeness is drilled into you in the military and it's a hard habit to break."

"I guess there are worse ones." Shoring up her resolve and nerves, she ran her palms down her thighs as she said, "He's waiting for me at the house. Nice to meet you, Pete."

Pete nodded then surprised her by saying, "He's a good man, none better. I'd trust him with my life. Nice to meet you, ma'am."

She'd trusted Dan for years before ever meeting Gerard, maybe it was time she did so again. "Yeah, he is. Have a nice day, Pete. Take care of my baby." She waved her hand toward the filly and then strode out of the stables, having made her decision.

Pete watched the attractive brunette with the haunted eyes leave the stable, wondering at the grim determination that had settled over her face and what, or who was responsible for the nightmares that must have put that look in her eyes. God knows, there were more evils in the world than what happened during war, and he wasn't the only one who found the days difficult to get through.

Dan did his best to remain calm and unaffected as Nan entered his house and walked into the den with slow, measured steps and a curve to her mouth that set his pulse to jumping along with his cock. He recognized that brazen, teasing smile, but not the uncertainty in her eyes. The girl he remembered was still in there, wanting to re-emerge. Now, if he could just push the right buttons to help her find her way back, he could get the rest of the story.

Remaining seated in the wide recliner facing the stone fireplace, he let her set the pace, widening his knees as she stood before him. "Are you going to take me up on my offer, then?"

She went to her knees as gracefully as always and looked up at him with that small grin still in place. "It'll be weird calling you Master here, but," she trailed those long fingers up his thighs, "this is the same no matter where we are, right?" Cupping her palm over his denim covered cock, she squeezed, her smile spreading to reveal straight, white teeth.

"Right." Her eyes remained uncertain instead of sparking with pleasure, but those soft lips kept their curved shape. She wasn't comfortable with the situation, not like she normally would be, but she still didn't hesitate to lower his zipper and grasp his heated flesh in her hand as she released his cock. The craving for dominance was still there, so Dan let her stroke him for a minute and enjoyed her tight grip moving up and down his rigid length until his blood heated to the boiling point. Aching for the familiar, pleasurable suction of her soft mouth and clinging lips, he fisted his hands to keep from reaching for her and instructed, "Mouth only for right now, Nan. Lace your fingers behind your head. That will help you keep from using your hands without triggering your fear by binding them."

Nan licked her lips, a slow sweep of her tongue over the lush curves that had him gritting his teeth to keep from climaxing right then. While Dan enjoyed the tease that reminded him of her old self, he didn't relish waiting for his pleasure. It had been way too long since he'd played with his favorite sub. Edgy arousal hardened the warning behind his one-word growl. "Nan." She rewarded him with her obedience, lifting her hands behind her head as a noticeable shiver racked her body that didn't alter her expression.

"Like this, Master Dan?"

With her hands laced behind her head, elbows out, the position pushed her full, unfettered breasts forward, their plump roundness shifting under her thin tee. "Yes, just like that." Wrapping his right hand around the base of his cock, he held his erection up and called on every ounce of his patience as he waited for her to dip her head.

Nan wanted to taste Master Dan again in the worst way, to feel his smooth crown bumping her throat as she took him deep. There was no fear, or even a hint of anxiety as she bent at the waist and swept her tongue over his seeping slit, savoring his pre-cum sliding down her throat. Without his hands or restraints binding her, she stayed in control. She dipped down and closed her lips around the thick girth, enjoying the way his size stretched her lips and filled her mouth. The memory of how his thick, long cock would burn as he slid inside her pussy, stretching and filling her the same way drew a shiver of remembered pleasure.

When her nose bumped his hand at the base, she pulled slowly back, swirling her tongue around and around, pausing to scrape her teeth over the bulging, pumping veins before traveling back up to his cap as Dan groaned above her. Nan basked in the contentment of pleasing a Dom again, of accomplishing a feat without bad memories intruding.

"You're as talented as I remember, hon, even without using your hands. Suck a little harder now… *ahh*, that's it."

Bobbing her head up and down put a strain on her neck and upper shoulders, but his approval made the discomfort worth it. The only thing that could make this scene better would be if she were naked, could feel his eyes and hands on her as she pleased him. Unbidden, the memory of the last time she'd been naked in front of a man popped up and drew a shudder of revulsion. Gerard had left her shivering and bleeding after his last visit to her in that dank, dark room before she'd been rescued, her body bruised and cold, her mind raging at him and herself for landing in that predicament.

"What's wrong, Nan?" Dan asked, the laser-sharp concern and underlying anger in his tone pulling her back to the present.

Nan shook her head, refusing to give up the treat of servicing him to the past. Putting all her efforts into getting him off, she focused on swirling her tongue faster over his hot flesh, stroked with harder pressure where she knew he was most sensitive. She scraped her teeth down the silk-covered shaft, his deep groan adding to the warmth generated from the simple task of seeing to his needs. Keeping her eyes down, she waited for him to grip her face and take over her movements as he usually did. When he didn't, disappointment swamped her despite the thrill of drawing out his release with hard suctioning pulls of her hollowed cheeks. His cock jerked, the spurt of his cum jetting down her convulsing throat, but she missed the sore throbbing of her warm buttocks from a long spanking beforehand egging her on. The flutters of arousal, tight nipples pulsating from the bite of clamps and a damp pussy aching to be pummeled remained absent, and damn it all to Hell, she wanted those satisfying sensations back.

As Nan swallowed the last of Dan's orgasm, she lightened up on her draws, loosening her tight lips clinging to his throbbing flesh as she lowered her hands to his tense thighs. She took a few seconds to enjoy licking the satin-smooth crown, removing every pearly drop of cum before lifting her head and gazing up at his flushed face. Fine tremors rippled under her skin as she saw the toll giving up control had taken on him in his clenched fists and rigid jaw. His hands gripped the armrests, the raw scrapes across his knuckles catching her eye.

Frowning, she licked the taste of him off her lips as she traced a finger over the cuts. "What happened here?"

"A purge of anger. Come here."

Dan reached down and hauled her onto his lap, wrapping his

arms around her. She'd never been a cuddler. Other than a few caresses to help her come down from an exultant high following an intense scene, she didn't desire comfort. Since she hadn't achieved that lofty goal, in fact hadn't experienced that ultimate ecstasy in almost a year, she didn't understand why his embrace felt so good, why she wanted to sit there longer when she knew she needed to get going.

"Just tell me one thing before I take you home, please."

With a sigh, Nan lifted her face up to his, knowing she owed him something for giving up his control to her, sensing from his tone and dark gaze he would battle her for an answer. "What?"

"Tell me you filed charges against the son-of-a-bitch."

That was easy enough. "Not to worry, Dan." She pushed off his lap before she let herself get too comfortable. "Thanks to his wealth, he's out on bail, but awaiting trial in August. I open in an hour and have to get to the shop."

Dan had never struggled so hard against anything as he did to keep from demanding more from Nan. The hunger for him to take over the scene, to exert his dominance, and her disappointing lack of arousal was written all over her face and in the dullness of her golden-eyed gaze. His lap and arms felt empty when she rose, but he would have to look more closely at that new reaction later. Pushing to his feet, he zipped up his jeans, wishing he could sit and enjoy the final clutches of pleasure she had pulled from him.

"Let's go, then." Clasping her hand, he led her out to his truck with one bright, positive thought pushing through his conflicting emotions. She hadn't cared for his passive role any more than he. That meant he could move a little faster with his plans to get her over the hurdle of her fears, which suited him just fine.

He drove her back to her place in companionable silence, and he was glad that hadn't changed between them. He couldn't think of another woman he'd been as comfortable with, either at a kink club or as a vanilla friend, than Nan. Pulling behind the tea shop, he didn't push her by insisting on walking her upstairs. The more he treated her as usual despite the temporary change in their relationship, the easier it would be for her to stay relaxed.

Leaving the truck idling, he turned in his seat and reached in front of her to unlatch her seatbelt and then open the door. With his face close enough to hers their breaths meshed and his arm brushed her breasts, he stated, "I'll pick you up for lunch on Wednesday since you're closed. Fair warning, I intend to up my control as well as pry more information out of you." She stiffened and narrowed her eyes, her mouth setting in a stubborn pout. "If you intend to balk or argue, call me and we'll cancel. You have to want this in order for me to help you."

Dan watched as his words sunk in and her shoulders relaxed, the pinched look around her mouth softening. "I don't plan to, but if I freak out while having lunch in a public place, I'll never forgive you."

He nodded. "Understood. That's not something I would risk, anyway."

"Then I'll see you in a few days." She hopped out, but before closing the door, turned back toward him and said, "Thank you for last night."

"I care, Nan, always have. You know that."

"I know, as do I." She gave him one of those cheeky, teasing grins he got a kick out of. "And that's why I'm not telling you to fuck off."

Slamming the door on his burst of laughter, he waited until she sauntered inside before heading back home in a much better mood.

Chapter 7

The craft fair brought in another good crowd that afternoon, and staying busy kept Nan from obsessing over what Dan meant by upping his control and wondering how far he would go in public. When at the club, she didn't mind letting go in front of others, in fact, she used to get off on the exhibitionism. Heeding Master Dan's commands in a public place was a different story. Before Gerard had destroyed her confidence in herself, she would have trusted Dan and herself without reservation. She regretted that loss the most, she thought as she locked the tea shop's door behind her after closing.

On legs leaden with exhaustion and with the headache she had woken up with starting to creep back in, she glanced around the town square still lined with booths selling everything from home baked goods to hand crafted items. She winced as she took in the milling, last-minute shoppers. The craft fair may have been good for business, but now all she wanted was the peace and quiet of her small hometown back. With a sigh, she wound her way along the sidewalk, the warm afternoon sun splashing down on her face helping to improve her mood. Early summer was a great time of year in Montana, and after months of frigid temperatures and snow, it was no wonder people were looking for reasons to spend more time outdoors.

Nan wondered what activities Greg and Devin offered at their new dude ranch, which is where some of these visitors had come from. She wouldn't mind checking out their resort, maybe spending a day trail riding and having a picnic in a scenic spot. That was, if she could face the two Doms again after her mortifying behavior the other night. She cringed whenever she thought of going back to the club, but giving up the lifestyle she loved and reaped so many benefits from wasn't an option. Regardless of her lack of trust in herself, she would rely on Master Dan to get her back to her former happy place.

She'd thought it would be difficult to switch into their Dom/sub roles outside of the club, the only place they'd indulged in them together. But the ease with which she had gone to her knees before Dan in his home surprised her as much as when he'd chosen to come to her last night instead of spending the whole evening at The Barn. Where their relationship would be once she was back to normal, she couldn't fathom, but at least his offer gave her something else to think about besides the nightmares.

Entering the library, she spotted Avery waving her over to a table. Books were spread out on the long, extra tables set up for the fair and several caught her eye as she padded over to her friend. "Have you been waiting long?" she asked, setting her purse down on the floor next to an empty chair.

"Nope, just got here. This is bigger than I'd imagined. Poor Willa is being run ragged. It's a good thing she has Alice, and a few other volunteers."

Nan glanced over at the front counter and saw Alice scowling before her face cleared and she smiled with a wave. "Alice appears a little harried also," she replied, returning the older woman's greeting.

"I don't think they were expecting such a big turnout, which is why we should take our time searching for what we want instead of bugging one of them for help. Okay with you?" Avery nudged her slipping glasses back up as she placed her purse on top of the table.

"Sure. The only thing I have waiting for me at home is a frozen Lean Cuisine dinner."

Avery eyed Nan's taller, thinner body with a frown. "Why the heck would you eat anything lean? Now, if you were as round as me, I could understand, but seriously."

Laughing, Nan started toward the book tables, Avery falling in step with her. "Honestly, I really like the food, it's that simple. You need to start listening to Grayson. Your figure is fine the way you are."

A red stain covered Avery's cheeks. "He said the same thing right before I left and wanted to change out of this dress. He also emphasized his point with the wooden paddle he's way too fond of using on me."

Memories, good ones, flitted through Nan's head as she envied her friend's good fortune. She would give anything to be on the receiving end of a hard, stimulating spanking again, one that would leave her butt sore and hot, so that when she sat or even walked, the discomfort would cause her pussy to spasm with dampness, a mind-consuming punishment that would erase the abuse Gerard had heaped upon her. The difference in her response to erotic pain as opposed to the excruciating agony she'd experienced those few days wasn't lost on her and was as unexplainable as her captor's actions.

"These look to be all suspense," Avery said as they checked out a few titles on the first table. "Let's browse here first. This is my favorite genre."

"Mine too, as long as there are some spicy scenes."

Avery flipped her a grin. "Don't we get enough of those in real life?"

She wished, and maybe, with Master Dan's help, Nan would have that again too. "Can you ever have enough?"

"True."

Nan was clutching six books in her arms by the time she'd browsed through all the tables and tiredness was seeping into her body and dragging her down. She left Avery to continue shopping and padded back to the table where they'd left their purses. Four books she intended to buy and two to check out, so she would need her card and wallet. Wondering if her library card needed updating, she set the books down and started to reach for her purse on the floor only to encounter an empty space. Swearing under her breath, she looked around and didn't see it anywhere. No one from Willow Springs would have taken it, but she should have remembered all these people weren't friendly neighbors.

Anger filled her as she calculated what cards she would have to cancel a.s.a.p. and the inconvenience she didn't need on top of everything else. She hurried over to the counter where Willa and Alice were ringing up sales and check outs, hoping someone had turned it in to lost and found instead of taking off with it. "Hey, Willa. I can't find my purse – I left it under a table while we looked around."

"Oh, dear, that's odd. No one would swipe it, would they?"

Nan could tell the thought distressed the eighty-something librarian as much as it did her. "Let me check the lost and found. Maybe someone thought they were doing a good deed, thinking it was left behind," Alice suggested as she patted Willa's shoulder. "What does it look like?"

"Thanks, Alice, that's what I'm hoping. It's brown leather, long strap and a front zippered pocket."

She returned in moments and shook her head in regret. "I didn't see it in there. I'm sure your credit is good enough we can go ahead and ring you up, isn't it, Willa?"

"Yes, dear, of course. I'll take care of it, if you'll announce closing time in fifteen, Alice."

"Will do. I'm more than ready to get off my feet." Alice went into the office behind the counter and as Willa pulled up Nan's card on the computer, the announcement came through the speakers. She came out balancing a stack of books and nodded with a smile before taking her load out to the shelves.

Nan shifted with impatience as Willa slowly put the information of each book into the computer, trying to keep from prodding her along. She knew how important it was to get those cards cancelled quickly and every minute could mean the hassle of another charge she would have to file against. She reminded herself the woman was doing her a big favor. By the time Willa finished and bagged the books, Nan saw Avery walking over to get her purse, which still sat on top of the table.

She reached for the bag. "Thanks, Willa. I'll come in this week and get these paid for."

"I know I can trust you, dear. I do hope your purse shows up, though."

Worry clouded Willa's already filmy eyes and Nan hurried to soothe her. "Don't fret. It'll just be a matter of cancelling a few cards and getting new ones. Thanks again."

She pivoted and met Avery back at the table, noticing she held even more books than Nan. Frowning, Avery asked, "What's wrong?"

"I gotta run, sorry. My purse is gone and I have to make some calls. I'll see you at our weekly tea gab." Nan dashed toward the front door before Avery could keep her any longer, but her friend's voice halted her halfway across the room. "Nan! It's right here."

Nan spun around, embarrassment washing over her face as she saw Avery lifting her purse from under the table, right where she'd left it. "I swear, it wasn't there ten minutes ago," she said when she reached her. Checking the contents, she was further chagrined to find nothing missing, not even her cash. Confused, she shook her head.

"Hey, relax." Avery reached over and squeezed her hand. "It's the same color as the carpet. You probably just missed it."

"Yeah, that must be it." But Nan knew that wasn't it. Her purse had not been under the table when she'd looked. Shaken, she followed Avery back to the counter where Alice had returned and now eyed her purse in surprise along with Willa. "Found it," she quipped, feeling like an idiot as she withdrew payment for the books. "Sorry about the hassle." Ignoring Alice's skeptical look and Willa's relief, she quickly took care of her purchases, told Avery goodbye and dashed out, hoping it was tiredness to blame for her confusion and screw-up.

As he did every morning upon leaving the house, Dan swept his gaze across the miles of acreage spread out before him, still marveling it was all his. His herd of Herefords grazed on the lush prairie grass, the half he kept as seed stock – cattle registered for breeding – keeping their young calves close. He spotted his four cowhands riding the fence line with Bernie keeping watch at the rail. Hiring the older, more experienced cowboy was one of his smartest moves, he thought as he strode over to him before heading into the office. What Dan didn't learn growing up on a ranch five times the size of his, Bernie had taught him.

Joining him at the rail, he leaned his arms on the top post, squinting his eyes as he caught sight of Tank's little offspring wobbling alongside her mother. "She's growing into those legs nicely," he commented, his lips twitching as the young horse frolicked with the energy of youth.

"She's going to be bigger than Zenia, and her coloring will be closer to Tank's black and white than her lighter shade. You still planning on giving her away to your girl?" Bernie flicked him a shrewd look from under his hat.

Dan pulled the brim of his Stetson even lower, although, why he bothered, he didn't know. Bernie always could read him like a book, not to mention he'd been calling Nan his girl for years, despite Dan explaining they were just friends. He left out telling him about enjoying Nan's submissive side at the club. His friend and employee may know about Dan's membership at The Barn, and what went on there, but Dan never revealed names.

"Maybe. Nan's thinking about it." Given the short time she'd taken to mull over his proposition, Dan figured she was already done thinking about accepting the gift in exchange for agreeing to his offer of help. He'd thought, given her independent nature aside from her sexual submissiveness, she might take longer to think it over. Her quick decision spoke volumes about how desperate her trauma had rendered her.

His gut cramped as his imagination conjured up the terror and pain of whatever that son-of-a-bitch must have done. Without the details, he could only guess, and he didn't like what he kept coming up with.

To take his mind off those thoughts, he nodded toward Pete and Morales, who were herding a few straying calves back to their mamas. "They seem to be working well now they've gotten the hang of things. Everything else going good with them?"

"As good as can be. Morales is adjusting faster than the kid, who I know has nightmares still. I do what I can, but it's a good thing he's still in counseling."

Bernie had seen more than his share of war atrocities in 'Nam, which was one of the reasons Dan had bonded with the older man so fast. His ability to cope without turning to drugs or even counseling spoke volumes about his inner fortitude. Dan hoped Nan's courage was half what his foreman possessed.

"I'll make sure Pete is forthcoming with the counselor. Thanks for letting me know. I'm headed into the office, but my schedule's light, so I'll be back after lunch. See you this afternoon."

"I'll be here."

"Thanks, Bernie."

Dan strode over to his truck thinking about the gift he picked up for Nan. Because her needs had always been better met with the application of a flogger, cane, belt or hand, he'd never used toys with her. In fact, didn't even know if she liked them. That was rather pathetic when he considered how many times they had paired up since meeting at The Barn. He looked forward to seeing her reaction to the bullet vibrator and prayed the powerful compact device would be effective enough she would be willing to give him answers in exchange for relief.

He never said he was not above using sexual blackmail to get what he wanted, and right now, he wanted nothing more than for her to tell him what happened to her in New Orleans.

Thirty minutes before Dan said he would pick Nan up for lunch, he texted her with instructions to wear a skirt, again leaving her to wonder how far he would go this afternoon in public. She'd spent the past two days looking forward to their lunch, anticipation fighting a never-ending battle with uncertainty until she opened the door at his knock and her body zipped into sexually heated overdrive. Her hopes for a positive outcome today soared from the welcome response to seeing him standing there in his casual attire of jeans and dress shirt, his tanned face shadowed by his Stetson. The only thing that could have made it better was if they were headed to the club with her dressed in her favorite lingerie or fetish wear instead of the simple khaki skirt and short sleeved topaz blouse. She didn't know how to act around Master Dan outside of the club.

"Hey, I'm ready," she greeted him, pasting on a confident smile.

"Not quite." Stepping inside, Dan kicked the door shut and fished a small package out of his back pocket. "There's the little matter of adding this to what I asked you to wear."

Nan swallowed to ease her dry throat as she recognized the butterfly shaped clit vibrator even though she'd never used one herself. She'd heard from others how powerful the small stimulator could be and didn't know if the heat enveloping her face stemmed from unexpected excitement or angry disappointment that he would attempt to push her that far in public. Before she could vent the latter, he laid a finger over her lips with a frown.

"Already you are not trusting me. I'm disappointed in you, Nan."

Instant regret shoved aside everything else. She'd never given any Dom cause for disappointment, except for Gerard, who didn't count as a respectable Master as far as she was concerned. In fact, she couldn't recall a time when Dan had expressed any dissatisfaction with her, either as a sub or a friend, and didn't care for the pang of guilt his words brought on.

"Sorry. This switch in our relationship isn't as easy to adjust to as I'd first thought."

He opened the package and pulled out the bright pink toy. "Let's hope it'll be worth it to you. Remove your panties, please."

It seemed he could adjust to the change much faster and easier than her. Nan's pulse skipped a beat as she reached under her skirt and slid her panties off, pushing them aside with her sandaled foot as he went to one knee before her. Extending the attached loops, he looked up at her and she could barely make out the dark brown slit of his eyes,

"Spread your legs and hold on to my shoulders as you step into the loops. I know we've never played with toys, but have you used the butterfly before, either solo or with someone else?"

"No, this will be a first." Nan shook her head as she braced her hands on Dan's wide shoulders and shuffled her feet apart before stepping into the loops. "I thought I was way past firsts." His muscles bunched under her palms as he pushed the straps up her legs and under her skirt. She bit her lip as he brushed his knuckles against her bare labia before his thumbs spread her folds. As he slipped inside her pussy and rooted out her clit, his touch felt more intimate here in her apartment than when he'd had his hands on her at The Barn. Heat coiled low in her abdomen as she held her breath against the gush of moisture his marauding fingers provoked. God, it had been so long since she'd enjoyed such a response. That had to be a good sign, didn't it?

"Breathe, baby, all done." Pushing to his feet, Dan brushed two damp fingers over her lips before strolling into the kitchen to wash at the sink. "How does that feel?" he asked over his shoulder.

Nan blew out a breath and reached for her panties, the butterfly covering her sex drawing her eye. Licking her lips, she shuddered with a suppressed moan as she tasted herself. "Weird on the outside, I can hardly feel it inside."

"You will. Ready?" Returning to her side, Dan grasped her hand and opened the door.

"For lunch, yes. For whatever you're going to ask me while that thing is buzzing, I don't know. Honest enough for you?"

"Yes. Thank you." He squeezed her hand. "But the buzzing won't come until you earn that pleasure. That should ease your mind a little."

Before she could admit it did, she took a step, the move shifting the butterfly tentacle over her clit, the tingle halting her in place. "*Oh.*"

Dan smirked as he tugged her down the stairs. "Told you."

She tried to adjust to the distracting sensation as they walked down to Dale's Diner and accomplished that feat well enough to pause at the door with an assertion of her own. "Just so you know, I'm not calling you Master outside of the club."

"I've always admired your independent streak as much as I've enjoyed your submissive side, Nan. But don't push me too far by dictating to me."

His displeasure, given in that dark tone, drew a quick tremble and another damp quiver inside her pussy, reaffirming what she'd been thinking. Agreeing to Master Dan's help was going to work, and she would have the gift of that filly and her life back on track soon.

"Belle," she announced as soon they entered the diner and he placed his hat on a hook.

Dan turned to her with a puzzled frown. "Belle?"

"That's the name I picked for the filly you're going to give me."

He nodded in approval as Gertie called out from behind the counter. "Just you two?"

"Yep, just us," he returned.

Gertie pointed to one of the smaller, corner booths. "Sit your butts over there. I'll be by in a minute."

A smile creased Dan's lean, weathered cheeks. "You gotta love that woman. Confident of yourself, now, are you?" he asked Nan as she slid behind the table and he took the seat opposite her.

"No, I think I'm more confident of you than of me. And don't let that go to your head," she warned.

"Wouldn't dream of it."

Nan wasn't fooled by his deadpan tone; she caught the brief grin twisting his mouth. Her attention shifted to his hand as he reached down into his pocket where he'd slid the remote to the butterfly and a second later a low hum buzzed across her clit. Even knowing it was coming, she still jolted at the sudden burst of fluttering sensation. Fisting her hands, she glared at him as she adjusted to the arousal the low, soft thrum produced.

"Relax. I know what boundaries not to cross. Feel good?"

"Yes, different and…" She sighed and reached for the glass

of iced water as heat spread up her core. After taking a drink, she admitted, "It's been a long time."

Leaning back in his chair, Dan turned the vibrator off and crossed his arms. "How long?"

As her body settled down, Nan breathed a sigh of relief and took another sip of water before revealing the mortifying honest answer. "Almost a year, not since before I went to New Orleans."

Dan's eyes widened in surprise and then narrowed in speculation, but before he could comment, Gertie arrived to take their order. "You already know chicken strips are today's special, so what do you want?"

"A smile first, Gertie. Come on, it won't hurt you," he cajoled with an engaging grin even Nan was hard pressed not to fall for.

Gertie bared her teeth but her eyes twinkled. Everyone knew how much she enjoyed her gruff reputation, and how caring and protective she really was of the people she'd known most of their lives. "Not all of us have cushy jobs we can take long lunches away from, Daniel." She looked at Nan. "You need something that'll put the weight back on you, girl. How about the special with extra mashed potatoes?"

"I haven't lost *that* much weight, but the special sounds good. I can't eat all that in one sitting, so bring a take home box too, please. Thanks Gertie."

Dan handed Gertie their menus back. "Make it two specials, but I won't need a box."

Nan smiled as the older woman walked away, calling out their order as she went. "She'll never admit to being a softie under that gruff exterior. I should know. I've tried to get her to." She hissed at the sudden return of pulsations against her clit, fisting her hands until he stopped them again a few seconds later. "Why do you keep doing that?" she grumbled, squirming on the seat.

"To give you hints of what it can lead to if you answer my questions to my satisfaction. Tell me how you met this asshole."

She toyed with her napkin as she replied, "At a BDSM mixer in a reserved party room at a popular restaurant. The public venue was safe enough, and my research into the people hosting it didn't unearth anything negative about them or their private club, which had a good reputation. What I didn't know was he was as new to the group as I." She shrugged. "That was just one of his lies."

Regret crossed his face. "Unfortunately, there are no safety nets out there against liars. I'm sorry, Nan. What did your brother have to say about you going?"

Nan shook her head, hating to admit her fault. "Another mistake I made. He was out of town and I was lonely and bored." *And thinking way too much about you, missing you way too much for my peace of mind.* In the aftermath of dealing with her trauma, she'd forgotten that until now. "I did call him and tell him where I would be that evening."

Barbara, the other waitress delivered their meals, and the laden plate she put in front of Nan looked so appetizing, her stomach rumbled in appreciation. "Enjoy you two," she said as she refilled their water glasses before shuffling off to the next table.

Someone cranked up the old-fashioned juke box as she dug into the mound of steaming, gravy smothered potatoes. "Oh, God, there's nothing like freshly made mashed potatoes."

Dan scooped up a large forkful of the creamy spuds. "Or French fries or hash browns. Clyde mentioned once he's here slicing and dicing potatoes by four every morning."

"*Mmmm*, remind me to kiss him in gratitude before we leave."

His lips twitched as he replied, "I'll do that." Cutting into a juicy, breaded chicken strip, his gaze sobered as he resumed his questioning with a frown. "You went to his place that night?"

"No," she returned sharply. "I wasn't that stupid. I agreed to meet him for coffee the next morning, at a bistro where we sat outside. We spent the entire next day touring the French Quarter and no, he didn't give off any strange vibes, not until I agreed to dinner at his mansion the following night."

Just thinking about that evening sent a wash of shame and remembered fear through her. Her throat went dry and she reached for the water, only to stop short of taking a drink when the tiny pulses resumed. "Jesus, Dan," she moaned, gripping the glass and taking a fortifying gulp. Every time he teased her with the toy, her frustration and ache for more inched up another notch.

"I want all of you here, with me, hon, not your mind back there." He turned the vibrator off as soon as she set the glass down and nodded. "Good girl." The simple praise warmed Nan where the cold had begun to return. "Eat before we continue. I don't want you getting too distracted or upset before you're full. Gertie was right. You've lost too much weight."

Nan scowled, irritated at the reminder, but their long friendship kept her from taking it personally. Biting into the juicy, breaded chicken, she glanced around at the lunch crowd, hoping he wouldn't delve much deeper with his questions while they were here. Nobody could hear them in the corner, with the music playing and noisy conversations echoing, but that didn't mean she wanted to tell him about Gerard's evil side with others so close, or even today.

Chapter 8

D an didn't care for the way Nan's face paled with his questions, or for the slight tremor in her fingers, and thought it best to table further inquiries until after they left the diner. Whatever memory had distracted her was enough to cause her distress, and that bothered him on a level he'd never experienced before. He caught signs of the woman he remembered whenever she teased him or refused to kowtow to him as she might at the club. She'd always given back as good as she gave, and he liked that about her. Which is why it hurt to see her cowed over a bad memory, and why his gut tightened in anger on her behalf.

Still, as he signaled for the check, he needed to know more before they got together at The Barn, with luck, this weekend. "Lunch is on me," he insisted when she reached inside her purse. "I asked you out."

In a flash, that spark of independence returned with her frown and tight jaw, amusing him. "That's not the way we've ever done it, and you know it."

Pushing back, he stood and took the check from Barbara with a thank you before grasping Nan's elbow as she slid out of the booth. "That was then and this is now. Don't argue with me."

She rounded on him as soon as they stepped outside. "And what's that supposed to mean?"

"It means, when you agreed to let me help you get past the mental block that fucking asswipe is responsible for, things changed, at least temporarily, between us."

"I didn't think you meant to take it that far. Preferring to pay my own way hasn't changed because of what happened. The only thing that has suffered has been my ability to…" She floundered and looked away from him as they strolled down the sidewalk.

It was the first time Dan could ever recall seeing her at a loss as to how to express herself, and another grip clenched his abdominals. "Let's discuss your inability to submit fully, to immerse yourself in the kinky activities you've always embraced and enjoyed. Answer one more question for me," he commanded in a tone he usually reserved for the club. She flicked him a wary glance out of those gold eyes as they reached the tea shop but didn't say anything. "Why didn't you undress for Masters Greg and Devin last weekend?"

Panic flared in her eyes, darkening them to the color of an old penny. Nan started to turn away, reaching for the door, but he turned her around with a firm grip of her chin, holding her face up to his. "No. Don't turn from me, don't hide and don't keep it inside. If you do, I'll walk away, and you can cope on your own." He didn't mean it; he doubted if anything could motivate him to let her work her way through this without him now.

A myriad of emotions crossed her face; alarm followed by testiness and then resignation before the tight set to her mouth softened and her lips curved in a way that caused his heart to roll over. "You always did know what buttons to push, *Master* Dan, you rat bastard."

No matter how much he wanted to, Dan refused to smile at

the taunt as he released her chin and settled his hat on his head. "And don't forget it. Well?"

She turned serious, sucked in a deep breath and blurted the last thing he expected her to say. "I have scars, two, and I wasn't… hey! Shit, what's wrong?"

Dan shook his head, noticing how he'd gripped Nan's upper arms, not tight enough to hurt, but fast enough to startle her. Biting hot fury whipped through him like an out-of-control wildfire, burning like acid and leaving him seeing red. *The fucker beat her bad enough to break skin, draw blood, leave permanent damage?* He couldn't concede it, couldn't fathom how anything so horrendous had befallen her and he hadn't known about it, hadn't been there to stop it, or help afterwards. Dropping his hands, he stumbled back, afraid his touch would trigger a God-awful memory, and he wouldn't be able to handle that.

"You can tell me the rest later," he rasped. There was no way he could take hearing anything else right now, not and stay sane. Reaching into his pocket, he pulled out the remote to the stimulator. "If you don't have plans this afternoon, come out to my place. You can give Belle her first lesson on a lead. Here." He flicked the toy on high and handed her the remote, watching as the jolt of pleasure shocked her into gasping a deep breath. "It's yours, a gift. See you in a little while."

He spun on his heel, needing an outlet for the aggressive wrath consuming him, threatening his control to the breaking point.

The shocked fury darkening Dan's face followed Nan as she dashed upstairs. She hadn't been ready to tell him about her scars or prepared for his volatile reaction. The memory of how she'd gotten them had cooled her body, but the spasming damp heat from the rapid, strong pulses beating against her clit wiped it away just as fast. But nothing could erase his stunned rage on her behalf as he'd grasped the extent of her ordeal.

She didn't want to tell him anything else, but also didn't want to disappoint him again, because she suspected now he would demand to know everything. The guilt over shutting everyone out for so long, including Dan, was enough to live with, and to make up for. He hadn't pushed her into agreeing to his proposal, just dangled an irresistible reward in front of her, so she would finish the sordid, horrific tale when he insisted.

By the time Nan reached her apartment and closed the door behind her, she'd shoved aside the image of Dan's face to concentrate on the arousal building to a feverish pitch from the butterfly. Leaning against the door, she slid a hand inside her panties, her knuckles brushing the wet crotch as she fretted over losing the lovely sensations before they could expand into a climax. She hadn't been this close to an orgasm is so freaking long, it was a wonder she didn't explode as soon as he had attached the vibrator.

She gave herself a pleasurable moment to slide under the butterfly and trace over her puffy, damp labia before working her way inside her slick sheath. Swollen, damp inner muscles clamped around her finger as her throbbing clit set off the first small contractions. Shuddering on a deep moan, she stroked in time to the pulses, relishing the gush of cream as the spasms increased in intensity and speed. Slamming her eyes shut, she gyrated and rode her finger, whimpering as an orgasm burst. Sparks of pleasure traveled up from her gripping pussy, tightening her nipples, drawing beads of perspiration and enveloping her mind in a nice, fuzzy euphoria.

Taking her time, she stroked her pussy through the lessening contractions as she worked to calm her breathing and pounding heart. Nan didn't realize she still clutched the remote in her other hand until the fog cleared and the soft pulses against her clit still continued. Turning it off, she breathed a sigh of relief as the lingering, throbbing ache of her abused nub slowly ebbed. Compared to the orgasms she'd achieved under a hard-edged Dom's painful commands, this one was just a small pop, but hey, she mused, pushing away from the door, she would take what she could get. And right now, she felt pretty damn good.

After removing the toy and washing up, Nan changed into denim shorts and a blue tee sporting a large teacup, the tea bag string hanging over the side reading 'tea shirt'. Returning downstairs, she slid behind the wheel, her body relaxed, her optimism restored as she drove out to Dan's place hoping she'd given him enough time to get himself under control.

As the neat, dark red, white trimmed buildings of the Shylock ranch came into view, Nan experienced a quick spurt of excitement. Parking in front of Dan's two-story log and cedar siding home, she slid out of her car unsure if it was the anticipation of spending time with Belle or more time with Master Dan she was looking forward to most. Her orgasm left her relaxed enough to shove aside worries over what his reaction might be to hearing more about her ordeal, and as she strolled toward the horse stable, she vowed to continue thinking along positive lines.

The scent of fresh hay and a soft whinny greeted her as she entered the dim, cooler interior of the smallest outbuilding and she spotted Pete and another man outside Belle's stall. The young filly caught sight of Nan, her ears perking up as Pete adjusted a halter around her head.

"I think she's grown in the short time since I saw her last," she said as she joined them. Smiling, she held out her hand to the dark-haired Hispanic next to Pete. "Hi. I'm Nan."

"I'm Morales. Nice to meet you," he returned with an engaging smile, squeezing her hand. "The boss said you would be out. He hasn't returned from his ride yet, but you can take Belle out to the corral, if you want."

"I'd love that. Pete, how are you?"

"Ma'am. I'm good. It's nice to see you again, and it looks like our girl here is happy to see you again, too." He stroked the filly's neck and she put her head over the stall gate, giving Nan a nudge.

With a laugh, she pulled a sugar cube from her pocket. "May I?" she asked the guys, figuring they would know the foal's diet.

Pete shrugged. "Sure, she likes her treats."

As Nan held her palm out flat for the horse to take the sweet cube, Pete clipped a lead to the ring dangling from the halter around her nose. Handing her the end, he stepped back and opened the gate. "Go on out that side door, which leads right into the corral. We'll be in here if you need help."

"Thanks guys." Beaming, she led her baby out into the late afternoon sunshine, Morales' voice reaching her before the door shut.

"Think she's the reason for the boss taking off the way he did when he returned? Damn, I've never seen him so pissed."

"Me either, but…"

The door shut, blocking the rest of Pete's reply, but Nan heard enough to know Dan hadn't calmed down by the time he'd returned to the ranch. With luck, his ride would give him the time and space he needed to work through the shock of her revelation. She had to remember she'd had months to come to terms with those scars, and how she got them, and she still couldn't cope well with the memories. As she moved to the center of the corral, let the long lead out and tugged Belle into walking a wide circle around her, she decided it would be in the best interest of her female friendships to reveal that ugly remnant of the abuse as soon as possible. They might not forgive her if one of them heard it from someone else.

Not that she didn't trust Dan, but if she agreed to hook up with him Friday night at the club, there was a much better chance now of her stripping naked than before she'd agreed to his offer of help. She sifted her fingers through her hair, pushing it back away from her face and tightening her grip on the lead as

Belle tossed her head, eager to pull away when she spotted her mama out in the pasture. Dan mentioned she'd finished weaning just two weeks ago, so it wasn't surprising she still wanted the comfort of her mother. Nan pulled with steady, gentle insistence until Belle settled down and then clicked to encourage her back into a slow walk.

"I know, sweetie, it's hard being away from mommy, isn't it?" Sixteen years had passed since Nan lost both her parents, and she still missed them. The only thing she could be grateful for now was they'd been spared knowing about the trauma she'd endured. Shaking her head, she tilted her face up to the sun, letting the heat wash away the cold chill her thought provoked. She didn't want anything to mar the enjoyment of getting acquainted with Belle.

Dan reined in Tank as he spotted Nan in the corral with Belle. Slowing the steed to a trot and then a walk before pulling him to stop, he and Tank's chests heaved with their labored breathing from the vigorous ride and effort it had taken to reunite a stray calf with its mother. He hadn't planned on working when he'd lit out across the pasture, but when they'd come across the problem, the physical exertion turned out to be a welcome diversion from his thoughts.

His first inclination upon returning to the ranch had been to release his rage on his punching bag again but didn't think his bruised knuckles could handle it. A shiver racked his body as he eyed her across the field, wondering about the torments she'd suffered. Leaning his forearm on the pommel, he let Tank graze as he enjoyed the view of Nan's long bare legs, as sleek and toned as the filly's. She'd succeeded in introducing Belle to the lead already, the young mare now trotting around her in a graceful circle even though she kept turning her head to seek out her mama.

Dan straightened on a deep inhale as Tank shifted under him. Hell, he swore, given his volatile reaction to her nightmares the other night and to learning about her scars today, maybe he wasn't the right man, the right Dom to help her through this. Maybe someone who didn't have a history with her, or a valued friendship would be better suited to aid in her recovery. Someone with more objectivity, like... *fuck it.* It didn't matter which name he picked; he didn't like the thought of turning her over to anyone else. Damn it, she was his, for now at least, and he would see this through if it killed him.

With a booted nudge, he prodded Tank toward the stable, and the woman who had succeeded in twisting him up in knots without realizing it. "She's looking good," he complimented her as he reached the rail and dismounted. "It'll be another eighteen months before we can start on saddle training and riding, but at the rate she's growing, she'll be a hand taller than her mama and a good hundred pounds heavier."

Nan smiled as she slowed Belle and met her halfway in the corral until the filly butted her head against Nan's chest. Even wearing a bra, the move jiggled the full mounds and Dan had no trouble recalling the softness of her lush figure. She laughed and opened her hand with a sugar cube, which promptly disappeared into Belle's mouth. Giving the saddle cinch a loosening pull, he tossed over his shoulder, "You'll spoil her if you keep that up."

"Good. She deserves to be spoiled. How was your ride?"

Necessary. He slid the saddle off Tank and tossed it over the rail before looking back and nailing her with a direct gaze. "Long and rigorous enough for me to settle myself down."

She blew out a breath but didn't glance away as she replied in her forthright manner, "I'm sorry, I didn't mean to upset you. You are the one who insisted on knowing."

That tart reminder almost teased a smile out of him. Almost.

Before Dan could think straight again, he needed to see for himself the physical damage she was living with. "You're right. Let's turn these two loose and put our gear up."

Nan flicked him a wary look as he hefted the saddle over his shoulder, grasped her elbow and led her into the tack room in the back of the stable. Since the stalls were cleaned and the stable was empty, he guessed Bertie had already given Pete and Morales another chore, which worked well for him.

Hanging up the lead, she turned to face him, one slim brow winging up with her wry look as he walked over to shut the door. "Why do we need the door closed and locked?"

Dan wished he knew if the pink tinge staining her cheeks came from too much sun or was a positive sign of anticipation. Tossing his hat on top of the saddle he'd placed over a wooden horse, he stalked toward her only intending to look at her back. "I need to see, here, where we're alone and you don't have to fret over anyone else looking." At her shaky nod, he took her shoulders and turned her around. "Brace your hands against the wall," he instructed, sliding his hands under her tee shirt and pushing it up.

"Dan…" She hissed as he slapped her thigh, one light swat as he watched closely for any adverse reaction.

When all she did was take a deep breath and nod, he reminded her, "Master Dan, here, or anywhere else when my hands are on you, or about to be."

Nan dropped her head between her braced arms, the pose submissive, her tone not so much. "Yeah, okay, but I should get a break until I can adjust to the new status of our relationship."

"*Mmmm*, I'll give that some consideration." The tips of two thin scars appeared at her lower back and hip as he rolled the top up, one inch at a time, until it bunched around her shoulders. Damned if his finger didn't shake as he traced over the first one that ran almost straight down from her shoulder blades. The second was more jagged, crossing the first about mid-back and snaking around to her hip. The rage returned, burning his gut, but this time he pushed it back with ruthless determination.

"I could kill him for this," he rasped in a low voice as he continued to brush over the whitened lines. "Slowly, painfully. I know ways. You learn a lot of stuff in the military most people can't imagine. Things you believe you'll never have need of."

"Sir." Nan swiveled her head to look back at him. "I wouldn't be happy with you if you did that."

"Don't you dare preach to me that two wrongs don't make a right," he growled.

"Oh," she drawled, "I wouldn't dream of it, Master Dan. But I would be very unhappy if my favorite Dom landed in jail instead of Gerard."

"That's his name? Gerard?"

She turned back toward the wall with a shake of her head. "I'm not revealing anything else right now."

The bite in her tone signaled she was serious, and he didn't push it. He'd rather ease the sudden tension between them. Trailing his fingers up to her bra, he released the catch with a quick, deft twist, the strap separating and falling away.

"You didn't need to do that to see the scars," she whispered, lowering her head between her arms again in a pose he liked.

"No, but necessary to do this." Leaning closer, Dan slid his hands around her sides and cupped her dangling breasts, brushing his thumbs back and forth over her nipples as he placed his mouth on one scar.

"Oh, God," she groaned in a voice that wobbled.

"No, just me, hon." Kissing his way down the straight scar, he kneaded her plump flesh, increasing the pressure against her hardening tips. The white lines didn't detract from the smooth, graceful look of her or from the way she curved right above her shorts. He knew the shape of her ass below that curve, the softness of her malleable buttocks, the way she used to push back or lift up in a silent plea for more. The longing to reacquaint himself with the rest of her body as he plucked at her nipples and licked over her scars couldn't be denied but had to be delayed until he was sure he'd gotten his unstable emotions under control.

"What did he use? A single tail?" Dan squeezed her nipples when she shook her head. "Refusing to answer is not an option, Nan."

"Fine, yes, a very thin one, from what it felt like."

He rewarded her by going back to plucking her nipples and tickling her side with the scrape of his teeth. "Didn't you see it?"

Nan's shoulders slumped, as if in resignation before she admitted, "No. The room was dark, and I... *Sir*." Her voice caught as she pushed her breasts into his busy hands.

Dan couldn't bring himself to question her further; the strain in her voice was enough to rein in the urge to keep after her until he heard the whole story. "Thank you." Releasing her breasts, he re-hooked her bra and lowered her shirt before turning her to face him. Cupping her face, he was pleased at the need reflected in those golden eyes. Lowering his mouth, he laid his lips on hers, added pressure to get her to open and wasn't surprised when she resisted and pulled back with a confused frown.

"We don't kiss, or never have. You know that."

"That was then, this is now," he repeated before kissing her again. This time she let him in, welcomed his tongue and returned his strokes as her lips moved under his. By the time he pulled back, her eyes were swirling with frustration. Perfect. Keeping her guessing, and on edge was key to being successful this weekend when they met at the club.

Stepping away from him, Nan frowned and fisted her hands on her hips. "You're confusing the hell out of me, Dan."

"Am I now?" Slinging an arm around her shoulders in their familiar hug of friendship, he ushered her out to her car. "Since you insist on relating your story in bits and pieces, I'd say we're even on frustrating each other." Opening the car door, he leaned on the top as she slid in. "Friday afternoon I'll be helping with some of the prep work for the county fair, which is coming up way too fast, but I'll be at The Barn by nine. Does that work for you?"

Those soft lips curled up at the edges in one of her teasing smirks. "What if I already have plans with someone else, since you didn't exactly ask?"

"Break them," he returned before shutting the door and striding into the house without looking back.

"Do you think they're an item?" Morales jerked his head toward Dan, who was walking Ms. Meyers to her car.

Pete took the nail he held between his teeth and positioned it in the corner of the water trough. "I don't know, and it's none of our business," he replied, driving the nail into the wood with two rapid hits of his hammer. "But she sure is taken with the young one."

"Yeah. It was fun to watch them together." Handing him another nail, Morales surprised him with his next question. "You had another nightmare last night. Handling it okay, *mi amigo*?"

Pete jerked, forcing in a deep breath before answering. He had hoped neither he nor Bertie had awakened during his tossing and turning. Would he ever quit hearing the screams of his wounded and dying comrades? "Yes." He nodded without looking up and drove in the last nail. "I'm sorry if I disturbed you."

Pushing to his feet, he watched Ms. Myers drive away. She appeared more at ease today, with fewer shadows under and in her eyes. God, he prayed she continued to recover from whatever ordeal she'd endured to put them there. He knew first-hand how the memories could haunt you to the breaking point, how hard it was to function day in and day out, get through each night with nightmares of pain and suffering filling your head.

"You didn't. Let's take a break. I could use a soft drink and there are still donuts left from this morning," Morales suggested.

Pete laughed, as he was sure his friend had intended. The combined sugary sweetness of pop and donuts would give them a sugar high for sure, and he figured that was Morales' plan, better that harmless indulgence than Pete risking another lapse that would get him booted off the ranch and land him right back in prison.

"You're on. Dibs on the chocolate long john."

"Fuck, man, you don't think Bertie left any of those, do you?" Morales laughed as they strode into the small barracks.

Pete returned his grin. "One can always hope."

Instead of that scene bringing back the memory of the lash cutting into her back, the searing pain as her skin split and the metallic smell of oozing blood, Nan drove home with her back still tingling from Dan's fingers and lips, her nipples still throbbing from the tugs and twists. She trotted up the back stairs to her apartment with an ache for so much more, a euphoric high she could only achieve submitting to a Master's dominance. She was close, at least much closer than before, and that put her in a fabulous mood. So much so, she answered Jay's call as she entered her apartment in a sing-song voice of happiness.

"Hello, brother of mine. How are you on this beautiful day?"

"Who are you and what did you do with my sister?" he demanded, his tone laced with amusement.

"I am your favorite sibling who is going to be the proud mama to the most precious Appaloosa filly. You will *have* to come up here and see her. I've named her Belle." Tossing her purse on the sofa, she frowned when she spotted her breakfast plate sitting on the kitchen counter. She could have sworn she put it in the dishwasher this morning.

"Really? And when is this grand adoption taking place?"

Nan picked up the plate and placed it in the dishwasher, the clear memory of having already done so once coming back. Ignoring the shiver of unease racking her body, she answered without shying away from the truth. "As soon as I respond to Master Dan's control again. You remember me talking about him, don't you?"

"I remember he was one of your friends I talked to a few times after you asked me to field your calls, and that he was none too happy about my evasive answers to his questions." Jay paused before asking with concern, "Are you sure you're ready, sis?"

"Shit, Jay, it's been *months*!" She threw herself down on the sofa, now irked with him. "If not, then I'll never be."

"Okay, okay, don't get testy. How about if I give you some more good news to make up for my skepticism? Gerard lost his last bid to postpone the trial further. It's set for August first."

"Thank God." Leaning her head back, she breathed a sigh of relief. She wanted nothing more than to get the ordeal of testifying over and done with.

"I thought that would please you. How about I make a trip up there in a few weeks? Will that give you time to win that foal in whatever wager you have going with your friend?"

"If not, I won't be winning it. Thanks, bro. I can't wait to see you."

"Me too. Later, sis."

Nan shoved aside the unanswerable questions about the plate and went to poke through her club clothes. Friday would be here before she knew it.

Chapter 9

Yawning, Nan made her way downstairs the next morning with less than thirty minutes to spare before it was time to open. She never overslept, but for the first time in too long to count, she couldn't blame her restless sleep on nightmares. Just the opposite, in fact. Having Master Dan's hands and mouth on her again worked like a charm to reawaken the cravings he was so good at producing, and the need for more of what she knew he could deliver. God, she loved those feelings, the heightened sensations that begged to be expanded upon. The only thing putting a damper on her enthusiasm for returning to the club tomorrow night was fretting over the possibility she would freak out again. The humiliation of last week's debacle still haunted her. Another mortifying episode like that might be the final deterrent to ever getting back to her old self.

Noting the time as she entered the tea shop and stepped behind the counter, she shoved aside worries she couldn't do anything about right now and turned to start the brewers. Her hand halted before pressing the on switch on the first one, her breath stalling when she saw the lit-up green light and felt the heat along the side of the machine. "I turned it off, I know I did," she muttered, unease raising goosebumps along her arms. From her grandmother's first invitation to assist in the shop, she had drilled into Nan the importance of checking and double checking everything was turned off before closing up for the day. She'd *never* forgotten, not once in all these years.

"I must be more stressed over everything than I thought." Trying not to let that get her down, she flipped on the other pots then reached for the cabinet that held the gourmet coffees that were such a hit. Opening the door, Nan shook her head in disbelief at seeing two bags of tea leaves sitting on top of the ground coffee. Since she didn't want the teas smelling like coffee, she'd made sure to keep them in separate cabinets. Did she toss those up there by mistake? She didn't know how that could be possible; upon opening the cabinet, it was easy to see the stacks of labeled coffee bags as well as smell the rich enticing flavors.

Swearing under her breath, she snatched the teas down and stashed them in the correct cabinet before lifting down the coffees. After getting two pots brewing, she flipped the sign to open, the sight of several customers waiting to enter lightening her frustration over the strange mishaps that greeted her first thing this morning. Thank goodness her patrons were chatty and kept her hopping for the next hour, so busy she ran out of morning pastries and donuts before ten o'clock. Making a note to add to her order from the bakery for the weekend, she took advantage of the first lull to sip on her own cup of French vanilla roast as she propped open the front door to let in a fresh breeze.

"Good morning, Nan," Willa called out from across the street as she unlocked the library and Alice lifted a hand in greeting.

"Morning, Willa, Alice." She waved back, thinking again how lucky they were Alice volunteered to help out. The town didn't have the funds to hire anyone, and Willa wouldn't be happy if she didn't have her beloved job. Opening the library just a few days a week helped the city's budget and gave the older woman enough hours to keep busy without being too much.

Tamara pulled up just as Nan spotted Avery and Grayson getting out of his cruiser in front of the city building. Her throat tightened as she watched the sheriff pull his wife to him for a long, deep kiss, his hands wandering down her back to trace over her buttocks. By the time he released her, Avery's face was flushed. Since Nan preferred playing the field to being tied down with one guy, she'd never envied her friends' committed relationships. But an unaccustomed frisson of longing hinted something might be said for being the sole recipient of such a possessive, loving look as the one Grayson leveled on her friend as she walked toward the tea shop.

"He is so fucking hot." Nan nodded toward Grayson as Tamara joined her on the walk and they waited for Avery to reach them.

"Yeah." Tamara sighed. "Makes it hard to give up being single."

Nan laughed so hard tears streamed down her face. "You're such a liar. You went after Connor for years, ignoring every other guy who looked your way."

Tamara giggled. "Okay, you got me there. But I can still look and fantasize."

"About what?" Avery wanted to know as she strolled up to them.

"About your husband. We were just mentioning how hot he is," Nan teased her.

Avery's brows dipped behind her black frames, but her lips twitched as she replied, "Keep it up and I'll set my sights on Master Dan. I saw you leaving The Barn with him last weekend."

Tamara shook her head, turning to enter the tea shop. "Sure you would. You wouldn't sit for a week. Nan might enjoy that, but neither of us would risk such a punishment."

Nan followed them inside, wishing she could agree with them. There'd been a time when she'd not only relished, but embraced a painful session over a Dom's lap, and the lingering effects of such an intense punishment. But pining for a return of those pleasures wasn't the only thing clouding her head right now. For the first time, she experienced a stab of irritation over her friend's innocent remark about flirting with Dan. What the hell was up with that? Between the unexplained mistakes she'd encountered coming downstairs and now her uncharacteristic possessiveness, she would be lucky to get through the rest of the day without losing what remained of her sanity.

"So, did I miss something else this morning? Did we change our time to meet this week?" Their weekly get together at her shop was usually in the afternoon.

"No, we just didn't call you, figuring you would be here, regardless. I have a patient coming in at one today to make up an appointment and Sydney is at an auction with Caden," Tamara replied, choosing a table near the counter.

"And Gertie asked if I could fill in this afternoon for Barbara, who called in sick." Avery took a seat next to Tamara, glancing up at the chalkboard menu. "That cherry blossom tea sounds good."

"It is. Let me get it started."

As Nan strode behind the counter, Tamara called after her, "What did you mean, something else? Are you having senior moments already?"

Nan jerked as if struck then averted her face from Tamara's frown. "I must be," she tossed back, injecting a lighter note in her tone than she was feeling. "I seem to be absent-minded this week. First, thinking I'd lost my purse at the library when it was there all along and then this morning, discovering I'd left one of the pots turned on." She didn't dare mention the plate left out upstairs, or the misplaced teas. Her nerves were strung taut enough without having her friends hovering over her with concern.

Avery smiled and waved her hand in dismissal. "That stuff

can happen to anyone, at any time. You've been so busy since getting back, it's a wonder that's all you've forgotten."

"Not to mention still dealing with whatever happened in New Orleans, which we're still waiting to hear about," Tamara reminded her as she brought the cups over along with cherry scones.

Taking a seat, Nan was grateful they were the only ones in the shop at the moment. "I know, and I also know I owe you an explanation. I'd rather wait until there's wine and pizza though, and when Sydney can be with us so I don't have to repeat it."

"Okay, but let's make it soon. The fair is coming up. The Barn will be closed that Saturday night, so maybe we can get together then." Reaching for a scone, Tamara took a bite and moaned in pleasure. "*Mmm*, so good."

Avery sent Nan a wry grin. "That's what she said and sounded like when Master Connor bound her on the St. Andrew Cross last weekend."

Nan laughed, recalling only too well the pleasure of being restrained on the padded wooden X, her favorite apparatus. Damn it, she vowed tomorrow night would be different, she *would* get the relief she needed and *would not* let Gerard's torment of her interfere.

She hadn't counted on the torment of her own mind playing tricks on her. By the time Tamara and Avery left, the afternoon regulars were starting to come in and the rest of the day passed without much of a break. Nan was grateful for her loyal customers but getting back into the swing of working was draining after the months she'd spent doing little except wallowing in self-pity and nightmares. Before heading upstairs, she double checked all the brewers, ensuring each was turned off, and then did a quick inventory scan, making a note everything was put back in its proper place.

After fixing a salad for dinner, she tallied her books, called Jay for a brief chat and took a long, hot bath. Before turning in, she flipped on one light in the living area, the panda night light in the hall bath and her closet light in the bedroom, leaving the closet door halfway ajar.

So, why, when a sound startled Nan awake several hours later, did she find herself jerking upright in pitch blackness? With her heart lodged in her throat, nausea roiling in her stomach, she blinked to make sure she was awake, and with confirmation instant terror propelled her from the bed. *The door creaked, rousing her from a fitful sleep. Oh, God, he was back.* The flashback initiated a wave of frantic hysteria and sent her fleeing through the dark, dashing into the living room by memory since she couldn't see in front of her. "*Have you learned your lesson, cunt? Are you ready to behave like a proper slave?*" Gerard's cold voice rang in her head and she rammed into the sofa. Crying out, she stumbled her way to the door where she struggled with the lock. By the time she wrenched it open, her shallow breathing had switched to panting sobs, one questioning plea bouncing around inside her head. *Dan, where are you?*

Heedless of her scanty nightwear of satin boy shorts and matching camisole top, Nan ran through the moon-lit shop and dashed out onto the walk, shaking with relief at the bright glow shining from streetlamps. Leaning against the wall, she sucked in deep breaths, pressed a hand to her pounding chest and worked to get herself under control. But nothing stemmed the flow of steady tears or slowed her racing heartbeat. Burying her head in her hands, she shuddered as she realized it wasn't a power outage that caused her lights to go out, as her subconscious had been hoping.

Nan was so lost in her misery, she didn't hear the footsteps approaching and jumped when the deputy lightly touched her arm.

"Nan, what's wrong? Are you hurt?" Concern colored his tone as he looked behind her into the shop.

"Jase, I didn't hear you. Sorry." She'd known him since grade school and yet felt like a stranger standing there in her underwear pajamas, crying and trembling without an explanation. "I… needed some fresh air. I didn't think anyone would be out."

"It's my turn at taking the night shift. Are you sure you're okay? You look upset. Can I help you back upstairs?"

He reached for her elbow but she jumped back, not afraid of him, but of returning to the dark. Without thinking, she whispered, "I can't go back up there. It's too dark." Her voice caught, and she shook her head, as if that would clear the cobwebs of fear.

Jase frowned and looked up at the apartment's front window. "Forgot a nightlight, huh?" He smiled, trying to make light of her ridiculous statement, but she could see the questions clouding his face. "I'll run up and turn on some lights for you. Uh," he glanced sheepishly at her clothes, "why don't you wait inside the shop. It'll only take a minute."

"Thanks, Jase." Nan didn't care at the moment if she appeared a pathetic mess—she wasn't going back up to her apartment until it was well lit. Five minutes later, she thanked Jase and closed the door behind him with a new fear hovering in her mind. She knew she had turned on the lights before bed, just as she was sure she'd turned off all the brewers the other night and put her plate in the dishwasher the other day. God help her, had the stress of her kidnapping finally broken her mind?

Nan was still shaken Friday evening but refused to let her worries and fears deter her from the course she'd set out. Given how many customers had asked her today if she was okay or if she felt all right, she doubted she would be able to hide anything from Master Dan tonight. Since she still hadn't a clue how the lights went out, telling him, or anyone else about it would sound crazy. Hell, maybe she was nuts, she mused as she rifled through her closet. So far, the only explanation she could come up with was either her trauma had affected her mental state more than she thought, or someone was screwing with her. The latter didn't make sense since she was home, spending her days with friends and people she'd known most of her life. And, to what end? There would have to be a reason, and she could think of none.

Shoving the unanswerable questions aside for now, she chose her favorite black leather corset and matching thong to wear under a sleeveless, blue wraparound dress that flowed around her knees in a soft drape. One tug on the tie and the dress would fall open, revealing the corset that cinched her waist and breasts with front ties, short enough to leave a peek of nipples and an inch of her lower stomach showing above the thong. Master Dan loved this outfit, and she was counting on that to keep her mind off her troubles.

As she dressed, Nan remembered her silent calls for Dan's help last night, the same as when Gerard held her captive. She'd never been one to cling, not to friends, family or a man, and she didn't know what to make of the way she'd missed him so much after being in New Orleans for a few weeks or why he was the one she'd cried out to when in such agonizing pain and terror. Their friendship and occasional Dom/sub relationship had lasted this long because neither wanted more, both of them happy with not taking it further.

"Just what I need, one more thing to question over and over," she grumbled as she checked the refrigerator for something quick to eat. Reaching for the carton of opened yogurt, she lifted the lid and wrinkled her nose at the odd smell. "Okay, not that." Setting it out to dump in the trash on her way out, she snatched a smoothie to drink on the way, picked up the stale yogurt and grabbed her purse at the door. Pausing, she turned to double check the lights were on. The apartment was well-lit, but as she locked the door behind her, she considered bunking at Dan's house again. Just in case her mind was determined to play tricks on her again. Tossing the yogurt in the alley trash bin, she settled behind the wheel, refusing to allow any negative thoughts to intrude for the rest of the night.

"Nan!" Avery and Sydney rushed to greet her as soon as she entered the playroom, their distressed faces irritating Nan. "Grayson told me what happened last night. Are you okay?" Avery gave her a quick hug while Sydney eyed her with sympathy.

"I'm fine," she bit out, trying not to let her annoyance show. Why hadn't she considered the deputy might give a report to his boss, the sheriff? "I woke startled when the lights went out and freaked. I already feel like an idiot for overreacting, so let's not make a big deal about it. Please?"

Sydney nodded and squeezed her arm. "Sure, but next time, call one of us. You know we'd come out."

Nan rolled her eyes as they settled at a table. "I'm sure your husbands would just love for you to jump out of bed at three in the morning and make the thirty-minute drive into town to hold my hand because I got scared of the dark."

"Hey, what are friends for? Besides, Grayson would insist on driving me, so you'd get double the support." Avery grinned but Nan found nothing amusing about that possibility.

"I need a drink." Something strong to settle her nerves, which had kicked up yet another notch as soon as she arrived. Nan warmed to the activities already taking place, like the blonde she didn't know at the table next to them who slid off her Dom's lap and settled between his legs, bending her head to take his erection in her mouth. How could she not go damp as the girl's deep suctions reminded Nan of the taste and steely hardness of Master Dan's large cock? But the fear of another public failure along with the lingering stress of the previous night kept her on edge and irritable.

"I'll get them," Avery offered. "Beers?"

"I'll take a whiskey, straight. Thanks."

"I'll wait a bit, thanks, Avery." Sydney turned to Nan as Avery nodded and padded to the bar. "Who do you have your eye set on tonight?"

"I promised Master Dan I'd wait for him." She didn't reveal their bargain; that was between the two of them.

Sydney's grin turned sly. "You two have been seeing a lot of each other."

"Don't go making more of it than it ever has been," she returned. "We're just getting caught up with each other."

"Does he know more than we do about New Orleans?" she asked bluntly.

Nan sighed and tried to rein in her impatience. She was fucking tired of evading questions about her ordeal, as tired as she was of everyone asking. She wanted to let what happened in New Orleans stay there, but that wouldn't be possible until she got over it.

"Uh, oh, you're getting pissed. I can tell by that look." Sydney held her hands up in mock surrender. "No more questions. Let's just have fun. Starting with me going upstairs to keep Master Caden company."

"Sorry, Sydney, I'm tired from little sleep last night, is all."

"Here you go." Avery set their drinks down and looked toward the doors. "And just in time, from the way Master Dan is coming straight over here."

His timing sucked, Nan thought with a stab of irrational bitchy crossness. She wanted to finish her drink in peace before he took her over, and considering she'd just been hoping he wouldn't be much longer, she realized what a contradiction that was. Maybe she should have stayed home after all.

Dan drilled her with a dark-eyed look as he placed one hand on her nape in a gentle but firm hold. "Good evening, Avery, Nan."

"Master Dan. How are you?" Avery answered when Nan remained quiet, scowling into her drink.

"Good, thank you. Problem, Nan?"

The smooth, rich timbre of his deep voice held a note of steely determination that sent Nan's hackles up. Sliding him a coy glance, she drawled, "Not a fucking thing, Sir. Just trying to enjoy a drink with a friend, *alone*." She had no idea what had gotten into her. Her determination not to let the odd occurrences plaguing her deter her plans seemed to have deserted her as soon as she heard others knew about last night's incident. Exasperation with her whole fucked-up life, and those who kept insisting on hearing about it, made her down the alcohol in one throat-burning gulp.

His tight squeeze on her neck heightened her awareness of him, and what he expected of her. She shivered, a delicate ripple of longing for something she couldn't define, which added to her annoyance when he sent Avery away.

"Avery, hon, would you excuse us, please?"

"Sure, Master Dan." Rising, she flicked Nan a wary glance before returning to the bar where Grayson was bar tending.

"Why did you do that?" Nan snapped, slamming the empty glass on the table as Dan took Avery's seat and leaned back with a nonchalance that didn't fool her. His rigid jaw and dark frown had her thrusting her shoulders back in a defiance even she didn't understand.

"Because I want to discuss why I had to hear from Grayson about you standing outside in the middle of the night in obvious distress, and because your attitude needs addressing."

"There's nothing wrong with my attitude. If you don't like it, go order someone else around." Nan's chest tightened as she issued that statement. She wanted his help, needed his dominant control to snap her back to where she'd been before Gerard had stripped her of everything. So why was she trying to drive him away?

He started to rise, saying, "Belle will miss you if you're reneging on our deal."

Panicking, she jumped to her feet. "Wait!"

Sitting back down, Dan raised one brow and cocked his head, his face remaining impassive as he asked, "Are you backing out of our bargain or not, Nan?"

She pictured Belle's large, soft eyes and the months ahead of watching her grow followed by years of enjoying her beauty and company. Then she thought of Gerard's cold smile, the evil in his black eyes, his taunts, telling her to give up, that he always won, always got what he wanted. *Not this time, damn it.*

"No, I'm not."

"Then come here." Dan pointed right in front of him as he scooted the chair away from the table.

Her heart thumping like a jackrabbit, Nan stepped forward, holding her breath as he reached for the tie at her waist and tugged. The dress fell open, goosebumps dancing across her skin as he took his time looking her over. Reaching up, he slid one finger under the corset, grazing her nipple, the casual caress potent enough to produce an ache for more.

"I'm not happy with you," he said as he slid the dress off her shoulders and let it pool at her bare feet. Looking at her, he grasped her hand and drew her over his lap. "I want answers, even if it means you stay in this position all night."

Nan landed belly down across Dan's hard, denim-covered thighs, a position she'd been in countless times before, and yet still felt new, scary and exciting all at once. She braced for the pain, praying for that hedonistic thrill instead of fear. His calloused palm glided over her buttocks left exposed by the thong, and she soaked up the pleasant sensations his touch stirred up. Low voices echoed around them, mingling with laughter, the music and the sounds of play resonating from the loft. She wasn't alone, or in the dark, the exhibitionism releasing a familiar sweep of excitement to tease her senses.

A light swat stung her right cheek, drawing a gasp at the sudden sting. He didn't pause before delivering a matching smack on the left, and tears pricked her eyes at the rush of pleasure from the soft ache. "Tell me about last night." Two more identical spanks landed on top of the first ones, still light enough to warm with a here-then-gone sting. "What frightened you, a nightmare?"

Nan shook her head, grasping the chair leg for added support as he delivered a harder swat in the center of her butt. "I woke up, and the lights were out," she blurted, needing him to continue but stopping short of admitting she was sure she'd left them on. She should have remembered how astute he was. Two much harder smacks jiggled her globes, the painful burn spreading to her pussy. *Yes!* The urge to crow in delight at the return of her usual response to pain was difficult to suppress, but she recalled how fast that pleasure changed last week and held herself back.

"Common sense tells me if you fear the dark due to your trauma, you would not have forgotten to leave lights on before going to bed." Dan aimed for the under curve of her buttocks next, putting more force behind the spanks, enough to push her forward on his lap.

Nan trembled as he paused to inch a finger under the thong and trace over her puffy labia, his touch on the sensitive flesh setting off sparks deep inside her core. She'd almost forgotten the pleasure of a burning backside, of picturing others eyeing her red, quivering butt, of lying face down throbbing for more. With a low moan, she shifted on his lap, the pressure of her mound against his rigid muscles sending another blaze of heat spiraling through her.

With a low curse, Dan pulled back and blistered her buttocks with a rapid volley of spanks, alternating between light and hard, stopping only to brush his hand across her throbbing flesh before resuming again. "You were frightened, awakening to the dark, with no explanation for the lights being out. Correct?"

"Yes!" she cried out, using every ounce of her concentration and control to fight back the ever-present fear waiting to ruin this blissful torment that was the complete opposite of what Gerard had subjected her to. It hovered, right there, on the very edge of her consciousness, with small flashbacks to that dank cellar. But this time, Master Dan's deep, commanding voice kept her rooted in the here and now, held her enthralled with the slow build-up of pain and a hint of pleasure pushing its way through.

"And you didn't think to call me today, talk to me, ask me to check out your electric wiring? Why, Nan? That is something you would not have hesitated to do before you went to New Orleans." He reddened her thighs next, the disappointment in his voice hurting her as much as his hand.

Would he look at her as if she were nuts if she explained the strange incidents this past week? *Was* she nuts, imagining things? Nan shuddered from not knowing the answer and yearning to stay right where she was, under his descending hand. When she remained mute on the subject, he sighed, tempering his swats until they ended with soothing caresses and another stroke over her damp flesh beneath the thong, the dissatisfaction she detected cutting her to the quick.

"Stand up," he ordered, his tone gruff, his hands gentle and supportive as he assisted her. He held her hips as she wobbled, keeping his eyes on her face until she got her bearings.

Nan loved the way her buttocks pulsed with heat as her head cleared of the rush of blood from her dangling position. Looking around the room, she grew even warmer as she caught several people eyeing them with smiles of approval. Damn, she felt good, calmer despite knowing Master Dan wanted more answers. Her pussy ached for attention, and that also felt fucking nice. The disappointment still etched on his face bothered her, but she was as close to her old self at this moment, under these circumstances as she'd been since her return.

"Did the fucking asshole restrain you?" he asked next, the question catching her off guard.

Her buttocks clenched as he shifted his hands from her hips to fill them with her hot flesh. His grip stirred the soreness and felt so good she found it easy to answer him. "Just one day after he locked me in the basement. He removed the ropes, daring me to fight him. I did, and that's when he used the whip."

"*Fuck*, baby," he muttered with barely suppressed fury, his hands tightening on her cheeks.

"It's over, Sir, and I survived," she hastened to assure him, hating the torment crossing his face, and that she was responsible for it.

"Is it?" Dan murmured, releasing her buttocks and drawing her arms behind her back. Shackling her wrists together in one hand, he pushed her one step forward, between his spread knees, with a guttural order. "Prove it." One hard yank and he ripped the thong off with his other hand, leaving her exposed from the waist down.

Not stopping there, he reached up and released the top three hooks of the corset, her full breasts popping free of the tight confines, her reddened, pinched nipples aimed right at his mouth. Wrapping his lips around one turgid peak, he dipped a finger inside her quivering pussy, swiveling a seductive dance around her engorged clit. The slow tease was at odds with his steely grip and threw her into a tailspin of escalating, explosive sensation. Nan whimpered with the assault, a torrent of pleasure building as he milked her clit with tight pinches and bit into her tender nipple. The dual stings added to the discomfort of her sore butt and she trembled, burning hot and wet with an escalating need for more, for him.

"Prove it," Master Dan repeated, switching to torment her other nipple. "Come for me, just me, right now." He sank his teeth into the tender bud as he plucked at her clit with tight pressure.

Finally, the pain encompassing her backside, throbbing in her nipples, morphed into a familiar sweet heat that stirred her arousal and took command of her senses as effectively as he'd taken over her body. Her pussy spasmed around his finger, a gush of cream dripping down her thighs as her hips jerked in tune with his now pummeling digits. First one, then two and now three fingers filled her sheath as he used his thumb to press harder on her clit. Writhing before him, she tossed her head back and rode his hand, relishing the burst of fiery explosions filling her vision with fireworks and embraced the encompassing ecstasy like a drowning man would a tossed life preserver.

Nan didn't care who watched or heard her, only about achieving this goal and pleasing her Master. By the time she came shuddering down from the exalted high, she lay sprawled on Dan's lap, gasping to catch her breath, his arms tight around her. Tears filled her eyes, and that shook her more than the orgasm. She never cried, wasn't a sub who needed to release stress or pleasure with tears. Blinking until they dried up, she stiffened her shoulders and gazed up at him, whispering in a voice harsh with confusion and desire, "Take me to the cross, please, Master."

Chapter 10

As pleased as Dan was with Nan's response, he didn't think she was ready for the cross, and what she would expect him to do to her on it. He still wondered about what happened with her lights, and the tidbits she kept tossing out about her abduction were enough to strain his control as well.

"You're not ready for more, hon. You can't bring up a whip beating that left scars and nightmares and expect me to use even a milder instrument, like a flogger on you." He slid a hand under her warm ass and squeezed one buttock. "That was just a hand spanking, and yes, I was harsher than I planned because of your response." Which had been as embracing and wet as the last time he'd had the pleasure of her over his lap and her soft, bouncing flesh under his hand. "Don't feel as if you need to push yourself because of one positive outcome."

"I'm not," she insisted, straightening and glaring down at him. "I can do this, I *need* to do this. If you won't, then I'll find someone who will."

"Fuck that." Dan tightened his arm around her as she struggled to rise. "You're pushing me, and I don't like it. You've never exhibited your independence with a Dom that I know of."

Those soft lips he'd only delved past once twisted into a taunting grin. "That was then, this is now. I'm tired of waiting, wishing and wondering. Damn it, I want my life back. Maybe, if I'm successful in that, I'll get my sanity back too."

He saw the moment she thought she said too much. "You're not crazy, Nan. I know you better than anyone else, except maybe your brother. Not only as a play partner here, but as a long-time friend. Even after what you've been through, you are the most grounded person I know, sure of what you want, and willing to go after it no matter what. Fuck, but I admire that about you."

She narrowed those golden eyes and cocked her head. "Enough to give me what I want now?"

Stepped into that one, didn't you, Shylock? It looked like she was going to force him to prove his point, damn it. Maybe she would surprise him again, like she just did over his lap. "Stand up." Dan patted her soft thigh, sighing as she jumped eagerly to her feet. Her quick enthusiasm slipped a notch as he made short work of removing her corset, dropping the black leather on the seat and gripping her clammy hand. "If I put you on the cross, you know I won't allow you to leave anything on. Like upstairs, now everyone down here will see your scars, will know you endured a horrendous ordeal."

Ignoring her pale face, he led her to a footstool in front of a small sofa. He watched her face as he unclipped the cuffs at his waist, noting the stubborn set to her chin as he drew her hands behind her again and secured them together at the wrists. "I see you didn't think of that." Brushing his palm over her nipples, he asked, "Change your mind yet?"

Nan shook her head, but Dan refused to let her get away with that. With a swift drawback of his right hand, he swatted her ass hard enough to propel her against him. Clasping her upper arms, he demanded, "Answer me, Nan. You know better than to give me a non-verbal reply to a direct question."

She didn't turn away, but gave him a direct gaze as she replied, "No, I'm not changing my mind." Leaning her head back with a haughty look, she added with a quiver, "Let them look."

Dan nodded and stepped back, releasing her arms and pointing to the stool. "Kneel up. You know the position I want. Face the wall."

There was no mistaking the flare of excitement that lit her eyes, or the tighter pucker of her nipples, but her lower lip still quivered with a noticeable touch of uncertainty before she sank her teeth into the pouty softness. Folding his arms, he didn't offer to help her with the awkwardness of getting into position with her hands cuffed behind her. She wouldn't expect help where he'd never given it before, not if she wanted to get back to where she'd been.

A titillating sense of satisfaction coursed through Dan as Nan settled back on her heels, her fingers brushing her ankles, her spread knees unfurling the puffy folds of her glistening labia. The damp, dark pink swath of her pussy drew his eyes and stirred his cock. He ran his fingers through his hair, hoping he wasn't pushing *himself* too far. His long dry spell was biting him on the ass, and not in a good way.

"Very good." He traced down one scar before pivoting and, spotting Leslie, crooked his finger for her to come over.

"Master Dan." Leslie's eyes widened as they landed on Nan's back, but Dan placed a finger across her lips, glad to see anger over her friend's suffering tightening her face.

"Would you ask Master Grayson for a bottled water for my sub and a beer for me, please?"

"Of course, sir. Be right back."

Dan turned and patted Nan's still pink buttocks as he moved in front of her. "You're holding up well. I'm proud of you, baby."

Her tense shoulders relaxed, and a smile blossomed across her face. He held a finger up, indicating silence and then turned to see Connor and Tamara approaching with the drink order he gave Leslie.

"We offered to deliver these for Leslie," Connor greeted him, handing over the beer.

"Thanks. I'll take that, Tamara, thank you." Opening the water, he held it to Nan's lips. "Lift up enough to drink and give your shoulders and back a break."

She accepted the drink with a grateful look, and as she finished, he leaned forward to lick the water dripping off her chin. By the time he glanced back at the other couple, both had noticed the scars and lost their amiable expressions.

"What the fucking hell?" Connor ground out in a furious whisper, his hand tight around his wife's. Tamara's face showed horror, her gray eyes swimming with unshed tears.

Like Leslie, Dan placed a finger over her lips, saying quietly, "New Orleans, and yes, the two of us are dealing with it."

"And who is dealing with the son-of-a-bitch responsible?"

Nan peered around at Connor, twin red splotches staining her face, a bold fierceness glittering in her eyes. "The courts, come August first."

Connor moved in front of her, cupped her nape and brought her face up to his. "You should have told us, at the very least, told your closest friends." He brushed the softest of kisses over her lips. "Thank God you're home, sweetie."

"Nan." Tamara reached for her friend, but Connor grabbed her, tugging her against his side.

"We're headed up to the loft to relieve Devin."

Dan looked back at Nan and knew she had won this battle. He just hoped she continued to win the war. "We're headed that way. If the cross is available, hold it for me, would you?"

"Sure thing."

As Master Dan escorted her across the lower floor toward the stairs with a hand wrapped around her cuffed wrists, Nan vacillated between chagrin over the revelation of her ordeal and the return of the electric buzz she always experienced when naked in front of a slew of onlookers. She'd never been shy; just the opposite. She had embraced public exposure with as much ease and pleasure as she had erotic pain and bondage. But that sweeping thrill didn't keep her from shying away from the thundercloud of fury swirling in Master Grayson's gray/green eyes or tuning out Avery's shocked gasp Master Dan silenced with a snap of his fingers. The truth had to come out, didn't it? Now that it had, they could move on and put it behind them, if she could just make it up the stairs to the dimly lit loft with her composure intact.

"You're surprising the hell out of me, Nan," Dan stated halfway up the stairs, his proud look warming her to her toes.

"Don't tell anyone, but I'm shocking the hell out of myself, too."

A deep laugh rumbled from his chest, drawing her eyes to the lift of his wide shoulders, the tightening of his biceps as he assisted her on the final step. "It looks like the St. Andrew Cross is all ours." Nan's fear of another lapse returned with a sudden cold chill that racked her body and drew his sharp gaze as they stopped in front of the padded cross. "Nan? Do we continue or spend the evening socializing? Belle is still yours, either way."

She gazed upon the apparatus and memories assailed her, good memories of scenes between her and her favorite Dom. Squaring her shoulders, she said in a strong voice, "We continue, Sir. Please."

"Good enough." Reaching behind her, he removed the cuffs. "We didn't discuss your safeword downstairs, and I apologize for that lapse. I'm so used to doing scenes with you without the need to go over safety measures, it slipped my mind. Do you want to use red, or do you still like panda?"

"Panda, and I didn't think anything about it, either." She relaxed and smiled. "I'm still comfortable with you, even dealing with all my shit."

"It's our shit to deal with now. Stand here a minute. I want to get something."

Nan watched him stride to the toy cabinet on the back wall, wondering what objects he would choose to add to the scene. When he returned carrying a packaged double dildo, her buttocks clenched and her pussy wept. God, it had been so long since she'd been filled with anything except despair, fear and anger.

"I see you don't object to the dual phalluses. I thought they would help distract you from bad memories. Face the cross, please."

Master Dan twirled his finger for her to turn around, giving her no time to second guess her decision, or to fret as he bound her wrists and ankles in a wide V in record time. Then her heart stumbled as he began wrapping her arms to the post using soft rope, stopping when he reached her upraised elbow. "Sir?" Nan jerked and her arm didn't budge. The extra binding rendering that limb immovable both alarmed and excited her, the odd combination of emotions leaving her confused.

Dan ran his hand down her back and over her tight buttocks; the light touch sparking a thread of anticipation. "Deep breath. You're fine." He did the same to her other arm, telling her, "I've left the ends loose. You can work your way out of the ropes if you want, but they're still secure enough to hold against minor resistance. One tug, and I can free you, Nan."

"Thank you, Sir." His foresight helped spur her arousal and settle her uncertainty.

Putting his face next to hers, he rubbed her trembling lips with one finger. "I've always been here for you, hon. You forgot that while you were gone. Now, quiet, unless you need to use your safeword."

To Nan's surprised excitement, she found herself relaxing against the cross as he bound her legs from ankles to knees, the snug ropes lending her security she didn't know she needed. A mellowness invaded her body as Master Dan caressed her, squeezing her thighs, ghosting his fingers between her buttocks, tickling her sides, cupping her breasts. He played with her to the point of growing frustration, stirring a hunger for more, building heat and longing everywhere he touched.

"I think you're ready for the dildos," he whispered in her ear as he squeezed her buttocks. With a sharp nip on her lobe, he stepped back, and she heard him tearing open the package.

She braced herself for the invasion of the toys, gasping as he slid the rounded ends past her openings, her juices easing the way into her pussy, a copious amount of lube aiding the insertion into her rectum. Pure, unadulterated lust infused her from head to toe as the dildos stretched and filled her one slow inch at a time. She groaned, rocking her hips with the full invasion, the move shifting the embedded phalluses to rub against long-neglected nerve endings starving for attention.

"Please, Master," she begged without even realizing it until the leather strands of his flogger snapped against her butt.

"Tsk, tsk, girl. I believe I told you to keep quiet. Concentrate on the toys, Nan. I'll go slow, but don't hesitate to stop me if you become afraid."

The warning behind his stern tone wasn't lost on her, and she focused her gaze on Sue Ellen, who was bound on the fucking swing in the corner, enjoying her master husband's switch. Soft vibrations erupted inside Nan, tiny pulses teasing her sensitive vaginal tissues and those hidden, taboo nerves in her rectum. Strips of prickling pain spread over her lower back, following without pause across her clenching cheeks from the kiss of leather. She fell into his rhythm as if it were yesterday that they were together instead of almost a year ago.

"So pretty, Nan," Dan breathed, unleashing the flogger across her butt with more force. "Striped red, your ass squeezing the dildo, your pussy dripping around that toy."

She shivered on a moan as he upped the ante and struck harder. Prickles turned into a sharper bite the same time the pulsations went up a notch inside her. Heat spread from her back down to her thighs, everywhere he struck the building arousal in her lower body spiraled upward, tightening her nipples and drawing beads of perspiration. Even though she kept her eyes open and pleasure infused her, the blackness started to inch forward as pain and arousal intensified together until she couldn't differentiate between the two.

"No," she whispered with an adamant shake of her head. "Don't come back."

Just as Nan's vision grew darker, Master Dan was there, his deep voice in her ear, his handsome, tanned face made more appealing with the waves of thick blond hair brushing his neck filling her vision.

"Stay with me, Nan, right here, where you know you're safe. Don't you fucking let him back in." He increased the vibrations tormenting her lower body, saying, "Concentrate on that, baby, and me, nothing else."

The order worked, clearing her head as her grit to fight the past returned in full force. She focused on his face, his dark eyes as she issued a demand of her own. "More, Sir. I'm good, I swear."

"You damn well better be," Dan warned as he stayed within her sight and snapped the flogger on her tender lower back again.

This time, Nan arched into the strike, embraced the heated pain, relished the sweet increase of arousal as he mixed softer strokes that did nothing more than tease the previous pain back to life with a few more blistering hard swats. Her pussy clamped around the dildo along with her rectum as small contractions gripped the phalluses and a gush of cream soaked the vaginal vibrator. Pleasure grew, blended with the burning pain encompassing her backside. She gyrated with the slow build-up, whimpered as the contractions grew stronger, bringing more pleasure, enough to sweep up to her breasts as the leather seared her tips with a well-aimed snap.

Nan lost her focus as a body-encompassing, mind-numbing climax burst free, the ecstasy obliterating the past months of struggle. Her pussy and ass convulsed around the toys, her pelvis writhing with the onslaught as bright colors lit up the darkness she'd lived with and feared for so long. Master Dan's choked-up voice breathed into her ear, his words adding another glow to the pleasure already racking her body.

"That's my girl. I knew you could do it, Nan."

Recalling his earlier doubt, she would have laughed at that if her mind hadn't already entered that blissful euphoric stage that left her floating on air. Even with her fuzzy head in the clouds, she recognized there were more hands than Master Dan's releasing the ropes and cuffs binding her to the cross.

"Why in the blue blazes of fucking hell didn't she tell us?" Master Devin's harsh voice sifted through the fog, followed by Master Greg's calmer tone. "We didn't know, Dan."

Nan shook off the guilt, unable to make out Dan's whispered reply, and then she was floating in his arms, his steady, calming heartbeat under her ear as the room shifted with his measured stride. The next thing she knew, she sat snuggled on his lap, a blanket tucked around her as the room slowly came back into focus.

Master Dan's deep, satisfied voice rumbled in her ear. "Welcome back. How do you feel?"

Closing her eyes, she concentrated on her body, feeling the lingering stings crisscrossing her cheeks, the burning throb of her nipples, the emptiness of her butt and pussy. "Good." She laughed and looked up at him. "Real good, Sir."

"I'm glad. Hold that thought." Dan inclined his head, and she looked around to see Caden standing there, a frown marring his rough-hewn face as he squatted before her, balancing his large frame on the balls of his booted feet.

Nudging his Stetson back, Nan winced at the censure reflected in his bright blue eyes. "I'm disappointed in you, darlin'. We've known each other a long time; you've been a valued member here since we opened. Shutting us out after going through such a horrendous time is not acceptable."

Razor-sharp edged guilt sliced through Nan, and she floundered for an excuse in the face of his displeasure. "I'm sorry. Some of what I was going through had to do with accepting responsibility for…"

"Stop," Dan and Caden commanded at the same time.

Caden looked at Dan and she felt his nod before the head Master and her long-time friend rebuked her again. "A woman is *never* to blame when she is abused by a man. You can sass, get physical or use poor judgment, he still has no right to harm you the way you were, no right to touch you against your will. Understand?"

She didn't dare say no, and deep down, Nan knew he was right. How many times had Jay said the exact same thing? She used her mistake in misjudging Gerard, in ignoring the few signs that had caused her a moment's hesitation as an excuse to keep her pain to herself.

"Yes, I think I finally do. Thank you."

He reached out and squeezed her hand, pushing to his feet and then gripping her chin to tilt her face up. "See that you do."

"I can't tell if he's still pissed or not," she muttered, watching Master Caden walk away.

"I think he intended to keep you guessing." A rumble of thunder signaled an incoming storm and she slid off his lap with a sigh of regret. His arms had felt so good around her, his wide chest a comfort to lean against. "I better get going. I don't like driving at night in the rain."

Her reluctance to leave him must have been obvious because Dan stood, pulled the blanket off and held out her dress to slip her arms in as he said, "Come home with me. I'm not comfortable leaving you alone tonight, not after what happened last night with your lights, and not after what I put you through tonight."

"You've put me through a lot worse, much more intense scenes," she reminded him as she tightened the belt at her waist. Without the corset and thong, the soft material brushed against her bare buttocks and breasts, the light touch enough to warm the tender stripes and pucker her nipples again.

"But not under these circumstances." He flicked a finger on one nipple with a small grin. "Besides, you appear in need of me still. Let's go, you can follow me."

Nan wasn't sure what he meant to do once they got to his place as they never fucked outside of the club, and now that he'd accomplished what he set out to do, brought her to orgasm under his painful administrations, didn't that mean their bargain had ended? He gave no clue to what he was thinking as he escorted her to the parking lot, not until they entered his house and he tugged her into his bedroom instead of the guestroom.

With a quick yank on the tie, the dress fell open again. Sheer giddiness coursed through her, tickling her abdomen as he pulled the dress off her arms and sent her bouncing back on his bed with a slight push on her shoulders and a crooked grin.

Spreading her legs in invitation, she quipped, "We don't fuck outside of the club, remember?"

Yanking his shirt over his head, his grin turned wicked as he shucked his jeans and boots and came down on top of her, covering her body for the first time with his full naked glory. "That was then, hon," he rasped, gripping her hands and shackling them above her head, "and this is now." With his free hand, he made short work of sheathing himself before plunging inside her welcoming pussy.

Nan laughed, but before she could say anything, he covered her mouth with his, swallowing her moan as her slick muscles clamped around his surging, steely cock. She orgasmed with the second womb-bouncing thrust and the intrusion of his tongue, the fast release shocking them both. On a throat-snagging cry, she arched like a bow under his pistoning body, her pussy convulsing around his shaft until the tremors dwindled to small clutches.

Lifting his head, he pulled back until just his crown remained snuggled inside her. "Damn, girl, slow down. Remember, I have eight years on you."

"Can't," Nan panted, lifting against him again as he surged back inside her. "You'll just have to catch up, old man."

"I'll show you old man," Dan warned. "Wrap your legs around me. This is going to be hard and fast."

Raising her legs, she rubbed her feet over his clenching buttocks before crossing her ankles at his lower back and tightening her thighs against his sides. "Just how," she nipped his corded neck, "I like it." As he rose above her to ram deeper than before, she licked over his brown nipples, his chest hair tickling her nubs. With a triumphant laugh of pleasure, Nan exploded around him again, loving his rough possession and all those muscles pressing down on her.

Dan struggled to hold back, but as Nan's wet, swollen pussy squeezed and massaged his girth for the third time, the friction proved too hot as she bathed his flesh with the slickness of her climax. With several more pummeling strokes, he spewed his seed into the latex, his whole body shaking from the exultant, spiraling pleasure ripping through him as he continued to pound into her tight depths. By the time he pulled back with excruciating slowness, dragging his spent cock along her still quivering nerves, their harsh, gasping breaths blew hot on each other's necks, their heaving chests lifting and falling together as his perspiration-damp skin slipped on hers.

The incoming storm that had followed them home burst open with a window-blazing streak of lightning, a booming clap of thunder and a pounding deluge of rain. Nan dropped her legs from around his back and he missed the tight grip already. "Give me a minute," he said gruffly as he stood. "You can use the bathroom as soon as I get rid of this."

She flicked a sleepy-eyed look of satisfaction toward the full condom and he spun away before he caved to the temptation to pound into her again. She took less time than him in the bathroom, and as she padded naked back toward the bed, he noted the tired shadows under her eyes. Holding back the covers, he invited, "Come on, baby, let's get some sleep. I know you have to get up early."

"I do," she replied, sliding next to him and curling against his side. "But this is weird. I haven't spent all night in a man's bed since college."

"Then I say it's past time. Close your eyes. I'll leave the bedside lamp on."

She stiffened and started to pull away but he tightened his arm around her with a warning growl. "Nan."

"I hate this!" she burst out against his chest. "I've never feared anything."

"Well, now you do. We'll deal with that phobia later. Now be quiet. If you're not tired, I am." That was a lie, but he'd say anything to get her to rest.

Ten minutes of silence passed with her breathing softly next to him, one long slender arm draped across his waist, her hand gripping his side as if anchoring herself to him. He thought she finally slept until her hushed voice interrupted the lull between thunderclaps.

"I met up with him three times, in public places before going to his house, and I let Jay know where I was going, who I was meeting."

Every muscle in Dan's body went taut. If she was willing to talk, he wouldn't stop her, even if he wasn't sure how he would react to any new revelations. "You played it safe, which is good. Think how much worse it could have ended if you hadn't."

Nan shuddered against him, her deep, indrawn breath pushing her breast against his side. "I know, I've thought of that. But I ignored my unease when he showed me his dungeon, which was both creepy and exciting, if that makes any sense. The first night at his house, he put me in the guestroom, another questionable move. I told myself he was going slow, being thoughtful even though I let him know I was interested in submitting. That lasted until he did everything to my body for two hours except allow me to climax or fuck me. After instructing me not to touch myself, he left for his room."

"You were pissed."

"Yeah, you know me, I'm not into punishments for no reason. I planned to leave in the morning. But when I came downstairs, naked because he'd taken my clothes, he was waiting on the veranda with a gourmet breakfast and a return of his charming demeanor."

When she paused, he took a stab at what came next. "It didn't last. He showed his true self."

"Yes. He ordered me on my knees and then revealed what he expected from his slave. After refusing to lick his damn shoes, I spent the next four days locked in a windowless bedroom, no food and only tap water in the attached bath to drink. I didn't know that would be the best part of that week."

Nan's soft skin grew cool and Dan pulled her tighter against him, his rage returning full force as the storm outside beat against the window. "You don't have to say anything else. I don't need details. Tell me how Jay got you out."

"That's easy," she said in a relived tone. "When I didn't contact him for over twenty-four hours, he tried calling, texting, leaving messages. Gerard confiscated my phone, and he answered the texts, but my brother saw through his evasive replies and returned to New Orleans as soon as he could. He said he went straight from the airport to Gerard's place, but Gerard insisted he put me in a cab a few days after I first arrived and he hadn't heard from me since."

"And he's wealthy, comes from old money and his family holds influence, right?"

"Right."

She nodded, and her hair tickled his nipple. Ignoring the small jolt of pleasure, he asked, "How did Jay get in then?"

"Determination and love. He browbeat his superior to get him a warrant, threatened to go it alone, even to quit his job if he didn't get help from his precinct. Since they needed him more than they cared about pissing off the Avet family, they sanctioned a surprise raid. Their timing was perfect. Gerard wasn't home, and when he returned, he saw the police cars and ambulance and kept driving, straight to his private jet. The bastard fled the country, and it took months to extradite him back."

Dan shifted on top of her, kissed her and then said above her damp lips, "Remind me to thank Jay." Rolling back over, he pulled her on top of him, spread her legs alongside his and pushed her head to his shoulder. "Go to sleep now. You have nothing to fear with me here."

Chapter 11

As soon as Nan fell asleep on top of him, Dan shifted her to the side and slid out of bed. He lied when he told her he didn't need to hear all the details of those days in the basement, and he would never be able to sleep until he filled in the gaps. Snatching up his jeans, he padded out of the bedroom, pulled them on and moved quietly downstairs and out onto the front porch. The rain still fell in a steady torrent and blew a light mist over his face and chest, but the cool dampness did nothing to smolder the heat of his anger.

He still had her brother's phone number from when he'd spoken with Jay after Nan quit answering his and everyone else's calls and texts. Disregarding the late hour, he sat down on the porch swing and pulled out his phone. Jay answered on the third ring, his irritable voice coming through loud and clear in Dan's ear.

"Do you know what the hell time it is? Who is this?"

"Dan Shylock, and yes, I know what time it is. I'm calling about Nan."

"What's wrong? Is my sister all right?"

Dan rushed to reassure him before getting right to the point.

"She's fine, sound asleep…" He paused before ensuring there were no misconceptions by saying bluntly, "In my bed."

"And you woke me at one o'clock to tell me that why?"

If Dan didn't know how close the siblings were, and didn't have Jay to thank for rescuing Nan, he would be worried about the silken note of menace in Jay's voice. "Because I care, a lot." And he was just now starting to realize what an understatement that was. "And because I've been helping her get over what happened to her in New Orleans, but I need to know more. Why is she so afraid of the dark?"

The rustling of sheets and low cursing resonated through the line before Jay replied, "She should be telling you herself, but since I know how stubborn Nan can be, and how she thinks she can get over those days on her own, I'll not only tell you, I'll send you pictures. You show them to anyone else and I'll come up there and yank your balls out through your throat. Are we clear?"

Dan winced, but understood where the other man was coming from. "Understood."

A jagged streak of white lightning split the black sky as Jay said, "We found her in a soundproof, locked room in the cellar, where he'd left her in the pitch black for three days. I am only going to forward three pictures, which will be shown at his trial. And I intend to talk to my sister tomorrow, Shylock, so you damn well better not be leaving anything out."

"I'm not," he murmured into the dead phone. Dan supposed he ought to be grateful Jay agreed to talk to him at all. The pictures came through seconds later, and his blood turned to ice. The one of her head and face, of the broken capillaries on her cheeks, her black, swollen eye, her blood-matted hair, shook him to the core. Fury built, threatening his composure as he scanned the mottled red and purple bruising along her ribs and abdomen, the split skin down her back.

Dan stabbed the delete button, erasing the images that would be forever seared into his brain. The desire to curb his rage with a six pack was quickly suppressed as he gazed out at the storm-lit sky. He knew from working with addicts who also had suffered trauma, like Pete, there was no escaping or erasing certain images through substance abuse, they would be there tomorrow regardless of what he did tonight.

What he did now, how he moved forward with Nan, depended on her. She had made leaps and bounds tonight at the club, surprising him, and he thought, maybe herself as well. But lapses were inevitable, and pushing for more too soon, could be more harmful than good. Unless she ended their bargain because she'd fulfilled her end of it by climaxing under his hand, and his body, he would let her set the pace for the next step. After having her again, he just hoped he could drum up the patience to go slow, if that was what she wanted and needed. Since he already ached to feel her slick cream bathing his cock as she squeezed another climax out of him, it sure as hell wouldn't be easy.

Nan roused from the most restful night she'd enjoyed in months, blinking her eyes open to note the time on Dan's bedside alarm. Crawling out of his warm, comfortable bed, she was grateful she didn't have to answer to a boss other than herself. That meant she could open up fifteen minutes late without anyone berating her. Still, she didn't like disappointing her customers, and there were a few who were already addicted to the gourmet coffees she'd added to the menu and showed up first thing every morning for their flavored caffeine fix.

As she picked up her clothes off the chair wondering where Dan was, soreness from the previous night's excesses made itself known with every move. Her vagina and rectum ached with each step into the bathroom and her skin still appeared flushed, her breasts tender to the touch as she soaped up in the shower. By the time she finished and dried off, she had no desire to add to her lingering discomfort by donning the tight corset again. Slipping the thong on, she wrapped the dress around her, enjoying the sway of her unfettered breasts as she skipped downstairs.

Nan caught sight of Dan out the glass front door, standing with Pete near her car. With his black Stetson obscuring a good portion of his face, she couldn't read his expression, but damn, he looked good in tight jeans and a worn, button-up work shirt with the sleeves rolled up to reveal the corded muscles of his forearms. Standing with his scuffed up, cowboy booted feet apart, he frowned as he looked down at the malnourished, scrawny kitten Pete held cradled in his hands. Her heart executed a slow roll as Dan reached out one finger and brushed the poor kitten's head in a compassionate caress; the same way he'd touched her last night as she'd spoken about Gerard's abuse.

She didn't know where the two of them went from here, but if the slow warmth spreading through her body and the tightness around her chest were any signs, she knew she wasn't ready for whatever this was between them now to end. There would be time to go back to their old relationships, enjoying each other at the club on occasion and socializing as friends outside of those evenings. Still, she would leave it up to him, she decided, stepping outside and drawing their attention away from the pitiful cat.

"Who do you have there, Pete? Poor thing looks as if she's lived a sad life so far."

"I saw a coyote stalking her behind the barracks last night and chased him away. Some food and attention and she'll be fine," he said, his eyes softening as he gazed down at the pathetic feline. "That is, if I can talk the boss into letting me keep her."

Scowling, Nan took up Pete's side. "Look at that face. Let him keep her and nurse her back to health."

"Do you know how many animals this makes he's adopted?" Dan shook his head, a grin curling his mouth. "But he was just putting you on, hon. Of course he can keep the cat. But," he turned a serious look upon his hired hand, "the squirrel's tail has healed. Turn that damned rodent loose or I will."

Pete chuckled, his face appearing younger and less strained as he smirked. "I already did this morning. As soon as I finish the chores, I'll take her to the vet in Billings and get her checked over." Nodding at Nan, he said politely, "Nice to see you again, ma'am."

Shaking her head, she waited until Pete was out of earshot before saying, "I've asked him to quit ma'aming me. I can't be that much older than him."

"You're not, it's the military background, and his own sense of courtesy." Dan eyed her with one of his probing gazes before asking, "How are you this morning?"

"Other than sore, I feel great. Thank you for the good night's sleep."

Taking her elbow, he steered her to her car and opened the door. "Come back this evening and let's see if we can make it two in a row. We'll stay in, order pizza, and I can see how rusty your pool skills are."

Her heart soaring, Nan beamed up at him as she settled behind the wheel. "You're on. Double pepperoni and I should make it by six or seven."

He nodded, tipped his hat and strode toward the stables, leaving her to drive back to town with butterflies tickling her abdomen and a feverish expectation humming through her veins.

Nan's upbeat mood lasted through the busy day as she conversed with her customers, more relaxed than she'd been since returning home almost three weeks ago. By the time the afternoon crowd dwindled, the last patrons waving goodbye as Tamara, Sydney and Avery entered, the lingering discomfort from the previous night's excesses had expanded into a full-body tired ache. The months she'd wallowed in self-pity and allowed Gerard's actions to keep her away from home and her friends had taken its toll on her stamina. That would be the next thing she planned to build back up now that Dan had succeeded in breaking through the ice that kept her from the lifestyle she loved for so long.

"I expected you guys much earlier," she greeted her closest friends, cringing inside at the mixture of censure and worry reflected on all three of their faces. Wiping her hands on a towel, she came around from behind the counter as Sydney flipped the door sign to closed. "So, now you know. Sit down and I'll treat you to a cappuccino from my new machine."

"Bribery won't get you out of talking to us," Tamara warned with a narrow-eyed glare.

"I don't want to get out of anything, but I won't rehash all the sordid details either. Between my brother, the D.A. and lately, Dan, I'm tired of reliving the ordeal." Carrying a tray with four steaming mugs, she took a seat at their table and passed out the hot drinks. "Please try to understand, and respect that."

"Well, hell, steal our thunder, why don't you?" Sydney grumbled, reaching for a mug.

Avery squeezed Nan's hand, her eyes pooling with tears as she said, "I'm so sorry for whatever you went through. I hope the bastard has paid."

"Not yet, at least not enough. I have to go back to New Orleans to testify at his trial the first of August. I knew if I didn't get back here and distance myself from the whole trauma, I wouldn't make it through the testimony."

"What are you willing to tell us?" Tamara asked.

Nan picked her way through the week-long kidnapping, touching upon Gerard's actions, and her own without going into a lot of the details. From the expressions of shock and outrage crossing her friends' faces, they were getting a clear picture without them.

"Okay." Pressing her palms on the table, Nan pushed to her feet and stated firmly, "That's it, and now it's time to move on. I have to return my library books and get out to Dan's." She wiggled her eyebrows with a wicked grin. "We're staying in tonight."

"You and *Master* Dan, or you and Dan?" Tamara wanted to know as they all rose to leave.

"I honestly have no idea, but I'll be happy with either. Now, shoo, and thank you. I mean it."

"No more secrets," Sydney admonished with a quick hug.

"No, no more." Nan didn't pay heed to the twinge of guilt tightening her abdomen. There was no reason to mention the strange mishaps occurring since she'd returned; she would figure them out soon without embarrassing herself by coming across as overreacting to a few misplaced items.

After locking up, she ran upstairs to grab her books and walked over to the library. She noticed there were only a few browsers still inside as she smiled at Alice behind the counter. "Hey, Alice. I'm glad I got over here before you closed. These are due."

Alice took the books, her brows dipping as her worried eyes ran over Nan's face. "Thank you. Are you feeling okay? You look a little peaked."

The older woman's voiced concern rang loud enough to draw a few eyes their way, and Nan tried to stifle her irritation by reminding herself Alice was just being nice. "I'm fine, just a little tired. It's been a busy weekend."

"Maybe you ate something that didn't agree with you," she prompted while cataloguing her returns.

Nan clenched her jaw, getting testy, wishing the other woman would let it go. She felt fine and didn't think she had looked bad at all when she'd glanced in the mirror before coming over. Reining in her impatience, she tempered her tone as she replied, "If so, it wasn't anything from my refrigerator. I just tossed several things, and all I've eaten today is a sandwich from the bakery, and I feel great. I need to get going."

"Oh?" Alice beamed, her curiosity switching gears. "Do you have a date?"

Nan wasn't sure what tonight was, but a date? She and Dan didn't date, but she wasn't about to reveal that to Alice. It was doubtful the newcomer knew anything about The Barn, or what went on there.

"Just an evening with a friend. Thanks. I'll come back this week, when I have more time."

"Goodbye, dear."

She waved, fishing her keys out of her purse as she exited the library. Walking into the back alley, toward her car, a soft, pitiful mewl snagged her attention, the heart-wrenching cry coming from the trash bin. Peeking inside, Nan sucked in a surprised gasp as she saw the scrawny tabby frothing at the mouth, trying to stand but falling against the metal side on wobbly legs.

"You poor thing." Unsure if the sick cat was friendly or diseased, she grabbed a towel out of the trunk of her car and wrapped it around him, trying to be gentle as she carried it to her car. The nearest veterinarian was in Billings, thirty minutes away, but she remembered Pete's medic skills, and the way he used them to help small animals. Making a snap decision to take the cat with her to Dan's, she settled him on the floor of the back seat and pushed the speed limit, hoping she didn't get a ticket.

Luck was with her as both Dan and Pete, along with Bertie, were leaving the stable as she drove up. "What do you have there?" Dan asked, strolling up as she lifted the towel wrapped cat from the floor.

Nan thrust the bundle toward Pete. "He was in my dumpster, in the alley. I don't know what's wrong, but he looks really sick."

Pete pulled the towel back and frowned, taking in the foam still bubbling from the critter's mouth. "That's a sign of nausea, maybe even poisoning. No telling what he got into. I'll try, but he's in bad shape."

Dan slung an arm around Nan's shoulders and Bertie offered

an encouraging smile. "Don't fret. If anyone can help the cat, Pete can. Kid's got a magic touch with animals."

"I hope so, but I don't want him to suffer."

"Softie," Dan whispered in her ear as he led her inside.

Nan rose above Dan and sank down onto his straining erection. He'd left the small bedside lamp lit again, and as he surged up into the welcoming clutches of her wet heat, he tried to remember how tender her swollen pussy still was. But hell, if this was how she wanted to set the pace moving forward, who was he to argue? Clasping her hips, he slowed her down, more to keep her from overdoing than to drag this out for him.

Too bad his cock still ruled. Within minutes of her rising and falling on top of him, of her juices easing his surging thrusts, her muscles contracting around his shaft and her mewling cries of pleasure mingling with their harsh breathing, he let go with a body-gripping orgasm.

Rolling to his side, he spooned her soft, damp body and followed her into a deep sleep. When he awoke next, mid-morning sun splashed across the bed, and his first thought was he could wake like this, glued to her, every morning. The idea he could be happy in a committed relationship didn't send him running; instead, he eased out of bed, slipped on his jeans and padded downstairs to put on a strong pot of coffee feeling quite content. He didn't know when his feelings for his long-time friend and sometimes submissive partner started to change. He recalled the irritation when she'd first ignored his calls while in New Orleans, followed by concern when her brother answered his texts. The signs of change she portrayed upon her return had set off alarm bells, but it wasn't until he'd seen her panic attack while with Greg and Devin that he'd experienced the first strange sensation gripping his chest.

Admitting to his feelings seemed to be easy, he mused as he got down two mugs when he heard the bathroom door shut upstairs. Which was surprising considering how content he'd been remaining unattached all this time. Figuring out how Nan felt now, and where to go from here would take some doing. Despite her struggles in coping with the trauma Gerard had subjected her to, his girl still possessed a healthy independent streak he doubted she would ever shed. When not playing, either in the club or anywhere else, that was fine by him; he'd never been drawn towards a twenty-four-seven Master/sub lifestyle. But she hadn't hinted at wanting to keep the changes his bargain made in their relationship, and given what she'd been through, he couldn't push her for more right now.

Nan entered the kitchen dressed in her shorts and top again and the memory of his legs entwining with her long, slender ones popped up. The girl walked around on a killer pair of limbs. "Good morning. Do you have time for an omelet before you go?"

"Sure. I don't open until one on Sundays, but even if time was short, for your omelet, I wouldn't hesitate to open late."

"A nice compliment first thing in the morning. You're in a good mood," he commented, pulling ingredients from the refrigerator.

"Two uninterrupted night's sleep in a row will do wonders." She hesitated as she sat down at the table before saying, "Thanks, Dan. I know it's silly, but until I can get a reasonable explanation for my lights going out, I'm not comfortable sleeping at home. You knew that."

He nodded, whipping the eggs and peering at her over his shoulder. "Yes, but I wanted you here, with or without your fears." Dan could see the tenseness ease from her slim shoulders. He admonished her by shaking a wooden spoon at her. "You should have known that."

"Are you going to use that on me?" she joked but her eyes lit with a spark of interest.

Shaking his head, he poured the eggs into a heated pan on the stove. "You are incorrigible. No, not today. I have to get to chores if I'm going to have time to check your wiring this afternoon." A few minutes later, he scooped fluffy cheese and onion omelets onto two plates and carried them over, taking a seat next to her. "I'll do some investigating while you're in your shop, then, after you close, I'll take you to the steakhouse." The pleasure turning her face pink gave him hope her feelings were slowly turning down the path his had already taken.

Dan pulled his truck behind Nan's shop an hour before she closed and, after letting her know he was there, he let himself inside her upstairs apartment and set about checking for the cause of the lights going out the other night. He hated thinking about her waking in fear, of the darkness resurrecting those days she'd spent in such pain and terror. It had been difficult enough for him to sleep just imagining it and he admired her determination to get over the trauma as much on her own as possible even though her stubborn independence could irritate him.

By the time he heard her coming up the stairs over an hour later, he still hadn't found anything wrong, nothing that would have caused the selected power failure.

"Well?" she asked as soon as she opened the door.

Placing his fists on his hips, he shook his head, his own frustration matching what was reflected on her face. "Nothing, hon. Sorry. It could have been a quick glitch, one we might not find. Are you hungry?"

Nan blew out a pent-up breath and forced a smile that didn't reach her eyes. "Sure. Give me a few minutes to wash up and change."

As she made to walk by him, Dan snagged her hand and hauled her into his arms. Watching her face closely, he fisted a hand in her hair and tugged her head back, the yank sharp enough to pull on her scalp the way she used to love. Those golden eyes widened and her pulse leaped under his thumb, but she leaned against him and welcomed his mouth on hers, proving those were positive responses.

By the time he pulled back, his own pulse had kicked up a notch and before he gave in to the need riding him to keep pushing, he released her with a swat on her ass. "Hurry up. I'm starving."

Things were changing so fast, Nan couldn't keep up. As she dashed into the bedroom for a clean blouse and then crossed the hall into the bathroom, she struggled to get herself under control. *This is a temporary bargain*, she chastised herself as she leaned over the sink and splashed water on her face. Dan wasn't giving any hints he was interested in making the change in their relationship permanent, or even wanting to explore the option. Both of them had spent the five years they'd known each other content and happy with their arrangement. He was the perfect Dom to meet her submissive sexual needs, and she counted him as one of her closest friends. She didn't want either of those things to change but, God help her, she now found herself more than willing to give a serious, one-on-one relationship a try. If only she knew how he felt. So far, other than his usual concern and the new touches of over-protectiveness he'd demonstrated, he treated her much the same.

Reaching for the towel, she dried her face and neck and opened the cabinet where she kept her make-up. Her hand froze in mid-air as she saw the mess a toppled bottle of foundation made. Swearing, she looked for the cap, positive she had screwed it on tight the last time she used it. It was not in the cabinet, and after a thorough search, she spotted it behind the toilet. Picking it up, her palm turned sweaty as she wondered how the hell it had landed on the floor with the cabinet door closed tight. She would never have put the bottle inside opened like that.

"I'm losing my fucking mind," she muttered, shaken by yet another unexplainable mishap. Grabbing a handful of tissues, she was almost done wiping up the mess when Dan knocked on the door, the sudden rap jarring her already taut nerves.

"Nan, hurry up or we'll have a long wait."

She flung open the door, snapping with annoyance, "I'm coming. If you don't want to wait, leave without me."

He looked from the wadded up, stained tissues to the cabinet and then back down at her before his damned astuteness kicked in. "Why are you so upset over a little spill?"

He wanted to know? Fine, Nan would spill the whole sordid story and see how fast he stuck around. Jabbing a finger toward the open cabinet, she bit out, "I would not have put an uncapped bottle of make-up back in the cabinet and left the cap on the floor. I put the damn plate in the dishwasher, I left the fucking lights on before going to bed and I did not misplace my inventory in the tea shop's cupboards. I'm so upset because apparently Gerard screwed up my mind as much as my body!" She flinched when she ended her tirade in a screeching voice but didn't back down in front of the dark disapproval in Dan's narrowed eyes.

With slow deliberation, he picked up her hand and yanked her out of the bathroom, hauling her into her bedroom without a word until he stopped by the bed and turned to face her. "All those things have happened since you got back, after we made our bargain, and you didn't think to mention them until now?"

Now, why did the soft menace underscoring his words give her such a thrill, send her blood rushing in a hot molten flow through her veins? As his hands went to his belt, that wide, black leather she hadn't enjoyed, licking with stinging force across her butt, in far too long, her pussy went damp and her buttocks clenched with the goosebumps racing across her skin.

"I don't know what's going on, what was I supposed to say?" she returned, licking her suddenly dry lips as he pulled the belt off.

"You were supposed to say, Master Dan, strange things keep happening, and I don't have an explanation for them. Pull down your pants and bend over the bed."

Heady excitement kept her from arguing, the ache to lose herself in the pain, to let it take her mind off her insecurities and fears, to turn herself and her problems over to him couldn't be denied. She didn't argue, didn't hesitate. With fingers that shook, she pushed her jeans and panties down, turned and went to her elbows on the bed.

"I'm disappointed in you, Nan." The first lash landed with a snap and a burning strike across both naked cheeks. "I thought you trusted me more than that." The next hit right below the first and pulsating heat bloomed in its wake. "We agreed to work together, I offered, and you accepted my help, agreed to my terms." The third sliced along the under curve of her buttocks and as the pain throbbed, Nan quivered in relief.

"I'm sorry. Please, Sir," she begged on a tortured breath.

"Please what?" he asked, trailing the leather over the stinging stripes.

"Please don't stop, not yet." The needy plea didn't embarrass her; instead, she relished the blistering snap of the next strike, cried out on the following one and whimpered as he delivered a last blow across her straining thighs.

"That's enough," he insisted, helping her up. Dan reached behind and palmed her throbbing ass, pressing her against his hard body. "I won't let you push yourself too far in order to escape." With a few squeezes that pulled a moan from Nan, he released her and tugged up her panties and jeans before returning the belt to his waist. "Now," he stated in an implacable tone she knew well, leading her back into the living area and pointing to the couch, "sit down and tell me when all this began, and don't leave anything out."

Dan paced in front of Nan as she told him about the odd incidents, her burning backside helping to keep her calm and focused, because, God help her, she yearned to believe this temporary arrangement between them could become permanent even though he'd offered no hints he was leaning that way.

"Wait a minute." He stopped pacing and held up his hand as she wound down. "All of this started *after* your purse went missing at the library?"

She frowned and nodded her head. "Yes, but I told you, my purse was there all along. Someone must have kicked it back in the corner where I couldn't see it at first."

"But, and just hear me out before you argue, what if someone snatched it long enough to make a copy of your keys? Doesn't the library still have that minute key kiosk in the back?"

Nan stilled as the slow burn of anger took hold. "Shit, you're right. But who would do that, and why? Everybody likes me, or used to," she insisted without conceit.

"Bored kids most likely, just screwing with you. I'll check with Grayson, see if there's been anyone else who has reported harassment. I can see that makes you feel better."

"It does," she replied, praying he was right and letting go of the anger. Changing her locks would be a huge weight off her shoulders, more so if the unexplained incidents proved to be from kids pulling pranks and stopped. So why, when Dan offered to install a new lock after dinner, and they headed out to spend another evening together, did she think that explanation was too easy?

Chapter 12

Nan left for Dan's early Wednesday afternoon, no longer able to wait to see him again. She knew she had only herself to blame for insisting on staying alone at her apartment after he had put on the new lock. At the time, she thought it best to distance herself from him, and her growing feelings that were escalating at a rapid pace after spending the night in his bed. Who knew how pleasant waking to a man's hard arms and legs wrapped around her could be? But, as she pulled into the drive at his house, she gave herself a stern lecture on keeping her wishes for this to continue to herself. Without a sign he would be open to making the temporary change in their relationship permanent, she refused to risk more pain to cope with.

As she slid out of the car, she looked around but didn't see anyone. The Dunbars and Grayson and Avery were invited to Dan's impromptu barbeque this evening, but she was over an hour early and didn't expect their friends for a while yet. She assumed Dan was working and headed to the corral where she spotted Belle grazing with her mama. Holding her hand out over the rail, she tried bribing her baby with a sugar cube, smiling when the filly recognized her and didn't hesitate to trot over.

"How's my girl?" she crooned, stroking Belle's silky nose, laughing when she nudged her arm up, searching for another treat. "Too many sweets aren't good for you, right mama?" Nan gave the mare some attention, enjoying the ripple of muscles as she stroked her neck.

"Are you spoiling her again?" Pete smiled, coming up behind her. "The little one has really taken to you."

"That goes both ways. I adore her already. You weren't able to help the tabby, were you?" She could tell by the way he averted his eyes he had bad news.

"No, I'm sorry." Pete hesitated, shifting his feet before asking, "Did you see anything harmful in the trash bin, something that could be poisonous if swallowed?"

Nan thought back but couldn't remember anything except smelly trash. The large container was used by all the shop owners on that block and was always half full. "No, but I didn't look. The last thing I dumped was a container of yogurt that was rancid. Oh, God, I hope that wasn't it!"

He shook his head, reaching out to squeeze her shoulder in reassurance. "No, that wouldn't have hurt him. He did show signs of poisoning, but it could have been any chemical not meant to be ingested, and he was malnourished to begin with. Strays don't tend to live long, so don't feel bad. You and I both tried, right?"

"Yes, but I'm still sorry. That must have been difficult for you." She knew Pete suffered a drug addiction at one time and that Dan had hired him upon his parole from a military jail sentence. His face still bore the ravages of his addiction and whatever trauma he had witnessed or endured while overseas that led him into it. After her own ordeal, her empathy for him, and the other young men Dan had tried to help over the years had skyrocketed.

"It's harder to watch them suffer. Dan is out in the west pasture unloading the cattle he purchased from the neighboring ranch. I can saddle Zenia for you, if you'd like to ride out to meet him."

Excitement shot through Nan with an electric zing that teased her senses. Both the prospect of a ride on the beautiful Appaloosa and a chance to observe Dan in cowboy mode galvanized her. "I would. Thanks, Pete."

Nan was glad she wore jeans as she mounted Zenia, Belle watching them with longing. Laughing, she reached down to tug on one ear. "Don't worry, sweetie. I'll be riding you before you know it." With a wave to Pete after he pointed her in the right direction, she urged the mare to take off at a brisk gallop.

The afternoon sun warmed her head and back, the breeze cooling her face as the ground below whipped by in a blur of spring grasses and bright field flowers. Tall Ponderosa pines separated the grasslands from the Douglas-fir forests, and if she looked closely, she might glimpse an elk or caribou. But it wasn't the vigorous ride and never-ending scenery that caused her heartbeat to thump wildly, but the anticipation of seeing Dan again, which told her how bad she had it for her sometimes Dom and long-time friend. Even though they'd spoken on the phone Monday and Tuesday, him calling to ask if anything untoward had occurred since Sunday, he'd been wrapped up in legal work in his home office until late in the evening the past two nights.

Nan pulled back on the reins as she spotted the long cattle trailer hooked behind a Dunbar Ranch truck in the distance. It was as easy to recognize Tank, Dan's stallion, as it was to pick him out between the other two on horseback. He sat a head taller and the back of his collar-length light hair showing below his hat glinted in the sun. As she trotted toward a copse of trees so as not to disturb them, her body hummed with a sweet rush of arousal pooling between her legs. She'd gone over ten months without sex while in New Orleans, and after two weeks of turning herself over to Master Dan, she was miserable going three days without his cock filling and stretching her pussy with his rough possession. Her flesh ached for the familiar burn of his palm or leather strap and the exultant pleasure it could bring her.

Settling at the edge of the trees, she sat and watched them unload the trailer, all the men wearing chaps that drew the eyes to their tight butts and crotches. "Damn, they can make a girl wet just watching them, can't they, Zenia?" Nan stroked the mare's neck, pining for Dan's touch again. The longer she sat there, the more she wanted him, and the more she realized how deep her feelings went. For the first time in her life, she was in love and wanted more from a man and a relationship than sex and friendship. But in all the years she'd known Dan, not once had he shown an interest in settling down to a committed relationship. In fact, before Connor and Tamara ironed out their problems, Dan and Connor were the two Masters everyone at The Barn thought would remain single.

Her heart twisted and with a sigh of regret, Nan turned Zenia around and rode back to the stable at a slower pace, trying to come to terms with the possibility she'd allowed herself to fall for the wrong man. No, she amended, the right man for her, just the wrong man to expect a return of deep feelings. She'd already agreed to go to the club Friday night with Dan, but after that, maybe she should consider ending their bargain, as much as it pained her to do so. She would not make another mistake by allowing this gaffe of falling in love to ruin their friendship.

As she rode up to the stable doors, Grayson and Avery pulled in. It took monumental effort to work up a smile of welcome, but Nan figured she'd better get in the practice of hiding her feelings for the next few weeks.

Dan nudged Tank around and watched Nan ride back toward the stables without coming over. Did she think he didn't know she was there? He was more attuned to her now than he'd ever been. Maybe because he'd missed her so much when her short vacation turned into a ten-month absence, or because of the way he had vacillated between anger and concern when she'd cut off all communication. Discovering he had taken their compatibility as Dom/sub when at the club and their otherwise easy, comfortable friendship for granted hadn't sat well with him. Neither had the nightmares plaguing his sleep since learning what had befallen her in New Orleans. Realizing how close he'd come to losing her, maybe never seeing her again, had left him shaken, and aware of just how deep his feelings ran.

Which was why he'd been so pissed when she'd insisted on returning to her apartment alone after spending two nights in his bed. No matter how much he'd wanted to argue, entice and demand she let him stay with her, he couldn't fault her determination to get her life back. Wasn't that what he set out to help her do with his bargain proposal? She was on a fast track toward that goal and that should make him happy, shouldn't it?

"Are you going to sit there staring all day or get back and start the grill?" Caden drawled as he slammed the back doors of the cattle trailer closed.

"He's mooning over his girl. I love it. Another one bites the dust." Connor smirked, tipping his hat back and looking up at Dan with laughter in his blue eyes.

Dan dismounted, replying, "Nan isn't interested in settling down like her friends." *But I might be.* Wouldn't that be a kicker, if, after all these years, he wanted to give a serious, committed relationship a try just to get refused by the only woman he could imagine himself being happy with for the long run?

"Are you sure?" Caden asked, cocking his head.

He thought of her insisting on going it alone to test the safety of the new locks he'd installed. "Yeah, pretty sure." He nodded toward the young heifers the brothers had sold him at a discounted price. "I appreciate the livestock, and the price."

"Once you start breeding, they'll add to your herd in no time. You may find yourself in need of more hands this time next year," Connor said.

"I don't have the time or the acres for too many more. My goal is to keep a certain head count and still have a profitable number to take to auction. Go get your wives and meet back at my place. Like you said," he tossed out as he mounted up again, "I need to get the grill going."

"We'll be there in fifteen." Caden waved as he and Connor got into the truck.

After riding over to Bertie and having a few words with his foreman, Dan kicked Tank into a full run, eager to spend as much time with Nan while she was still agreeable to their bargain as he could.

Tamara's look held skepticism as she asked Nan, "Are you sure that's all there is to it?"

"What else would there be?" Nan hedged. "You know me, and Master Dan. We're happy with the way things are." She picked up her beer and took a swig of the cold brew, hoping to wash down the lie. Her eyes kept straying toward the front doors of The Barn as she waited with damp palms and a rapid pulse for Dan to arrive. Other than the cookout on Wednesday, she hadn't seen him all week. They talked every day, and today he had wanted her to drive to his place and then ride out here with him, but she declined. Until she knew if his feelings mirrored her own, she didn't want to get too comfortable sleeping with him. Returning to her solitary bed after just two nights in his had been hard enough.

"Sure you are." Sydney shook her red head. "You two are as stubborn as Caden, and I didn't think anyone could match him when it came to fighting a relationship."

Avery grinned. "From what Grayson said, you two fell the fastest for each other."

As they bantered, Nan glanced again toward the doors, this time with an electric jolt sizzling through her veins as she watched Dan enter. The loud, pumping music faded to the background, along with the chatter and sounds of sexual activities reverberating around the cavernous barn as she ogled his sexy saunter straight for their table. His thigh muscles bulged under the snug denim with each long-legged stride and the black tee molded in a tight stretch over his wide shoulders and around his thick biceps. Without his hat, his wavy hair shone bright under the high rafter lighting, accentuating the darkness of his eyes and face, eyes that never looked away from her as he approached.

"Holy shit, girlfriend," Tamara breathed. "If you don't want him, I'll take him."

That ridiculous statement drew Nan's attention for a second. "Sure you would. Would that be with or without your husband?"

"Speaking as one who enjoyed the pleasure of a ménage once..."

"Hey!" Avery interrupted Sydney with a mock scowl. "What did I tell you about bringing that up? *Sheesh*, can't you forget you once had *my* Grayson's hands all over you?"

Sydney rolled her eyes, her lips twitching at Avery's mock outrage. "It was before you even came along. Hello, Master Dan."

"Ladies." Without wasting time, Dan grabbed Nan's hand and hauled her to her feet. "If you'll excuse us. I'm later than expected and would like to get a small matter taken care of before escorting my sub upstairs."

"What small matter?" Nan set all her reservations about her feelings aside and followed him over to the bar, her pulse tripping with excitement and a touch of apprehension. She couldn't read his expression or mood, but her body didn't seem to care. As soon as he'd wrapped his large hand around hers, her girly parts fired up on all cylinders, ready and eager for anything he wanted.

As they reached the bar, he pressed her back against the smooth oak edge, the thin sheath she wore with only a thong underneath offering no protection against his hard, muscled frame. Bracing his hands on the bar top behind her, he gazed down at her with a frown dipping his dark brows. "I'm not the only one unhappy with the way you kept me and your friends in the dark about the abuse you suffered in New Orleans. It was wrong of you to not only shut out everyone you've known for years, but to hide what happened, as if you were ashamed."

Nan winced at the censure in his tone and the hurt behind his words. "I'm sorry. I've had a lot to deal with, as you know, and…" She sucked in a breath as he reached for the hem of her dress and pulled it over her head, cutting off her sentence.

Filling his hands with her breasts, he asked coolly, "You were saying?"

"I forget." Arousal ignited as she leaned into his busy hands, loving the tight squeezes. Goosebumps popped up across her skin as he shifted his hands and gripped her nipples in a tight pinch. Her pussy clenched with each twist of the tender buds, each pluck drawing a fresh gush of cream.

"I brought you to climax once just from doing this." Dan pressed harder, his eyes never leaving her face.

Nan shivered and bit her lip as the pain sent sparks from her nipples straight to her pussy and wasn't prepared for him to release the tortured buds without warning. Blood rushed back into the abused tips with sharp, stabbing needle pricks, the hurt inflaming every nerve ending in her breasts. She fisted her hands to keep from releasing her frustration and gave him a narrow-eyed glare. "You won't do so again by doing that."

"I didn't intend to, at least not right now. You have a penalty to pay before we work on getting you over the last hurdle of your fears."

Before she could question him, he tugged her thong down, shoved it aside with one booted foot and lifted her bare butt onto a towel someone behind her spread on the bar top. A heated flush pumped up her excitement as those standing at the bar eyed Master Dan swinging her legs up, bracing her feet a foot apart and spreading her bent knees.

"Sir?" Fine tremors of awareness rippled under her skin as her body danced a jig of heightened expectation from his dark gaze.

Palming her labia, Dan leaned forward and brushed her mouth with his. "Thank you, Master Caden."

She swiveled her head and saw Sydney's husband standing behind the bar, reaching across her to hand a bottle of beer and a glass of ice water to Master Dan. When Dan set the water down and lifted his hand, she knew what was coming, and relished the burn of his slap on her tender folds. "One." He brought the beer to his mouth as he dribbled a few drops of ice water on her reddened, stinging skin.

"Oh, God." Nan groaned, leaned back on her hands, arching her head to gaze at the high rafters above. Dan bent his head and licked his cold tongue over her flesh, lapping up the droplets, each stroke stirring the heat building inside her.

As he raised his head, she caught Dan's nod right before Caden lifted his hand and delivered the next swat with his admonishment. "Two, and don't disappoint me again, Nan."

"No, Sir, I won't," she gasped with a full-body shudder as Master Dan again soothed her fiery skin with a splash of cold water and his tongue. Even though her entire crotch tingled with heat and throbbed with a sore ache, when Master Connor stepped up and landed his punishing blow, the sting was still less than what she craved, what she needed.

She shook, waiting for Dan to finish tracing his tongue over her hot skin, the scrape of his whiskered jaw against the chafed, delicate flesh drawing a mortifying mewl from her tight throat.

Swallowing her frustration, she accused him in a strained voice, "You told them to hold back."

"No, that's their doing," he denied, lifting his head and swigging another drink as Master Grayson arrived and gave her a granite-eyed look.

"I won't be so nice." The sheriff's blistering smack sent Nan's hips arching upward with a wrenched cry. "Dan said the bastard is awaiting trial. Good for you, sugar." He winked and walked away, joining Avery who waited by the stairs as Dan shocked her by plucking an ice cube from the water and applying it to her red-hot skin.

"*Crap!*" Nan's eyes widened as her skin numbed and then warmed under his soft tongue. A sharp nip on one pulsing fold brought her thighs together to press against his face. His deep chuckle vibrated up her quivering pussy before hard hands spread her knees again. Startled, she turned and noticed Masters Greg and Devin waiting to punish her next. "Uh, oh."

"Yes, I believe you know who is most upset with you. You put them in a bad position, hon," Dan said without raising his head from her crotch, his tongue dipping to trace up her damp seam.

She didn't know which felt better, that teasing glide or the soft strokes over her puffy folds that followed. Too bad he moved away before she could decide, she thought as first Master Greg and then Master Devin delivered blistering swats between her splayed legs, their disapproving looks stirring her guilt. "I'm sorry, Sirs," she whispered, surprised by how much she wanted their forgiveness. She wasn't used to disappointing Doms and didn't care for how it made her feel.

Devin skimmed his fingers over her inflamed flesh with a wink that helped ease her conscience. "You're forgiven. We don't hold grudges."

"Unless, of course, you make a habit of withholding important facts from us," Greg added with a flick of her left nipple.

The two men sauntered away before she could reply, and then

Master Dan's lips were ghosting across her reddened skin, his lips teasing the sensitive, swollen nerves as his tongue darted out to lap up the last splash of icy water. Once again, voices and music faded to the background as he used his fingers to spread her labia and delved between with his tongue. Arching against his marauding mouth, she let her head fall back further, basking in the sheer decadence of the position, the carnal act and the thrill of exhibitionism. Her sheath convulsed as he tugged on her clit with his teeth and plunged two fingers deep enough to bump her womb. Her arms weakened, sending her down onto her elbows with a soft cry as two words chanted over and over inside her head – *I'm back!* That happy cry ended on a frustrated curse when he pulled back before the tremors heralding her climax could erupt into pleasure.

Lifting her head, she exclaimed, "Damn it, why? I accepted my punishment and apologized."

Dan lifted her down and held her quivering, frustrated body close enough she almost forgave him. "Do you trust me?"

"Of course," she answered with irritation and a simmering need she feared only he could assuage.

"Then come with me and let's finish this."

Dan was as ready to burst at the seams as Nan, but not before they both got through this next scene. She'd been the girl he remembered just now, the naked submissive eager to please and embrace her pain-driven needs. As he tugged her toward the dangling chain and nodded to Greg and Devin who waited in the corner, he prayed he was as successful in helping her overcome the fear of darkness as he was her fear of pain.

Needy anticipation spread across her face as he lifted her hands to the attached cuffs and bound her arms above her head. Goosebumps popped up along her skin as he trailed his hands down the sensitive underside of her arms. "We agree you can trust me, right?"

She nodded, arching toward him as he cupped her full breasts and strummed her nipples with his thumbs. "Yes, Sir. I always have. You know that." Frustration underscored those last three words.

"Just reiterating before I do this." Reaching into his back pocket, he pulled out the silky blindfold and held it up. Immediate denial flashed in those golden eyes as she stepped back and her heel nudged the wall.

"I don't think…"

Dan stopped her with a finger pressed to her lips. "I don't want you to think, only feel, and trust. You have your safewords, and you know I'll honor them, even listen for them." He didn't wait for her to say anything else or give her time to fret over it. Lifting the soft, black cloth, he wrapped it around her eyes and then clasped her face, tightening his hands as he tilted her head back and took her mouth in a long, thorough kiss. Her low moan slithered down his throat as he dueled with her tongue, enjoying the way she matched him stroke for stroke as she pressed against him.

But her distraction from the darkness only lasted until he lifted his head. Dan could feel her heart pounding against his chest as her breathing turned to panicked pants. Putting his lips to her ear, he commanded, "Listen, Nan. Where are you?"

She bit her lip, straining to hear. He knew the second she caught Tamara's voice coming from the wooden A frame a few feet from them. "The Barn," she answered on a relieved sigh.

"Who are you with?" Taking his hands from her face, he traced down her back and gripped the rounded globes of her ass. "Who loves this ass, knows just how hard you like to be spanked, how much you enjoy anal play?"

A shiver racked her body. "You, Sir."

"Say my name." He slid a finger between her buttocks and teased her back entrance.

"Master Dan… *please*."

"Not yet." With a jerk of his head, Dan beckoned Greg and Devin over. "We want to make sure you're not thinking about any other place but here, nothing else or anyone else except us."

His friends wasted no time adding their hands and mouths to his as Nan gasped, "Us?"

Dan teased her mouth with his. "Yes. Master Greg and Master Devin want a chance to make-up for last time. You're not going to deny them that, are you?"

She might be a wimp about the dark still, but she wasn't an idiot, Nan mused. "Wouldn't dream of it, Sirs."

Master Dan's deep chuckle against her lips drew tingles down her spine, his praise sent heat straight up her pussy. "That's my girl."

Hands, so many hands, touched and teased, fingers plucked at her nipples and played around the seam of her aching vagina. Lips trailed kisses along her arched neck and suckled her puckered nipples. Teeth nipped, bit and scraped over her warming skin and tongues soothed the painful pinpricks left behind. Bright colors swirled behind the blindfold as pleasure spiked and arousal pulsed deep inside her womb, obliterating the darkness. Nan leaned her head back and jutted her pelvis forward, a silent plea for more. Deep, male laughs echoed around her, adding to the roaring in her head drowning out all other sound.

"*Shit!*" she exclaimed when those lust provoking fingers on her labia refused to slide inside her.

"Tsk, tsk." Master Greg's admonishing taunt followed with a slow, tight squeeze of both nipples that pulled a gasp from her and drew a drip of cream from her pussy.

"I think your girl needs a reminder of manners."

Nan recognized Master Devin's voice and assumed it was his hard hand that swatted her buttocks, but it was Gerard's cold tone she heard, his cruel words that penetrated. *I think you need a more forceful lesson on manners, slave.* Without warning, a quick flashback to that damp, dark cellar pushed to the surface, the memory of the fiery pain of skin splitting under the lash of Gerard's whip overriding the pulsing pleasure.

"Sir." The plea came out in a whimper and resulted in the immediate cessation of touch. Her frustration was followed by a sigh as she recognized the stroke of the thin crop down her back and Master Dan's voice in her ear.

"Where are you, Nan? Who are you with?"

His dark, commanding voice swept away the past and her misgivings, returned her to the present and resumed the pounding ache for more. "Here, with you."

"Yes, me." He snapped the crop across her buttocks, the quick slice of pain forcing her hips forward, right into the return of hands on her flesh.

"*Yes*," she cried in exultation as fingers thrust inside her with the next blistering slash. Hands molded the fleshy undersides of her breasts as two mouths covered her nipples and drew on the taut buds with strong suctions. Another stroke cut into the under curve of her cheeks as Greg and Devin pulled up on her nipples, elongating the tips before releasing them with a plop that shook her and the fleshy mounds.

"She's gripping my fingers," Devin's voice warned above her head as Dan struck her buttocks again. "If she gets any wetter or tighter, it'll be as she comes."

"Can't have that. Not yet."

Master Dan's words didn't penetrate the haze of arousal clouding her senses until he whipped off the blindfold as Masters Greg and Devin dropped their hands and moved back. Confusion and frustration had her gasping, "What?" as her freed arms dropped around Dan's shoulders and he hauled her against him, striding toward the stairs without comment until he reached the back sliding doors.

The sudden waft of cooler night air chilled Nan's sweat-damp skin until he bent her over the rail and sank into her pussy from behind. The first thrust resulted in an orgasmic burst of pleasure as he leaned over her and his deep voice whispered in her ear. "Welcome back, Nan."

One after another, multiple orgasms rolled through her, unraveling so fast they took her breath away, each as welcome as the sun after a storm. The pounding surge of climaxes matched the driving plunges of his cock, drenching her in sensation as her muscles squeezed and massaged his thick girth. Nan lifted her head and gazed out into the night, wondering where they would go from here, because, God help her, she didn't want this to end.

Chapter 13

Nan glanced at the time and groaned, rolling out from under Dan. "I gotta go," she said with regret. "I'm opening early and closing by noon for the fair."

Dan sat up and the sheet pooled around his hips, her mouth watering as she gazed at his thick chest and the swirl of brown curls she remembered tickling her nipples all night. "I have to get moving, too." Dissatisfaction darkened his eyes as he stood and hauled her against him. "We need to talk, soon."

A lump formed in her throat. Other than him insisting she return to his bed last night, he hadn't said, or hinted at where he wanted to go from here. With no other choice, she would take that as a positive sign until he said or did something otherwise. Nodding, she schooled her features to hide the flare of hope his words instigated. "I agree, but I don't have time now."

"Grayson and I volunteered our horses at the adult riding ring. Meet me there after you close."

"Sounds good." She leaned up and kissed him before grabbing her clothes and dashing into the bathroom.

To her relief, Dan was already out doing chores when she skipped downstairs and went to her car. By the time she was rushing upstairs to her apartment to change clothes, she only had ten minutes to spare before she opened at the time advertised for this morning. Pulling out her phone, she punched in the number to the diner and placed an order to go, wincing when Barbara replied it would be at least an hour due to the crowd.

"Okay. Just stick it under the warmer until I get there. I'm expecting a crowd, too. Thanks."

Nan's harried start to the day didn't get any better as the morning progressed. As much as she enjoyed her customers, and meeting new people who took the time to visit her tea shop before going to the fairgrounds, today she would rather be with Dan. She intended to tell him, point blank, how she felt, where she wanted to go from here with him, and only him. If he wasn't of like mind, she would deal with it. Her stomach cramped as she imagined going back to their prior relationship but she refused to think further on that possibility. *One thing at a time*, she lectured herself, carrying two filled cups over to a table.

"Here you go. I know you'll enjoy the cranberry orange," she told the older couple whose brand-new cowboy hats and western shirts screamed tourists.

"Thank you, dear. I just love this little town and can't wait to ride a horse for the first time when we get to the fair."

"You'll have fun," Nan assured her, unable to imagine never having ridden at that age. The bell over the door pealed and Alice entered carrying a to-go bag from the diner. "Excuse me," she said as Alice came toward her.

Holding up the bag, she smiled and handed it to Nan. "Willa and I were just finishing breakfast when your order came up. Since we were leaving and coming right by here on the way to the library, I sent Willa on and offered to run it in to you."

Nan took the bag with a smile of gratitude. "Thank you so much, Alice. I'm starving but couldn't get away yet."

"You're welcome. Will you be going to the fair this afternoon?"

"Yes, shortly. How about you?"

"I'm planning on it. Maybe I'll see you over there."

"Great, and thanks again," Nan said as a customer called for the check. Turning, she hurried to set the bag behind the counter, missing the satisfied smirk curling Alice's lips as she left.

It was over an hour later before Nan could flip the closed sign around after the last person left and she could load up the rest of the dirty dishes into the dishwasher. Her stomach rumbled, a reminder she hadn't taken the time to eat yet. Flipping open the lid of the Styrofoam container holding the order of biscuits and gravy from the diner, she grabbed a fork and scooped up a bite with one hand while reaching for another cup to put in the dishwasher with the other. "Oh, God, that tastes good," she mumbled. But before she could take another bite, a group of teenaged boys went running by, whooping it up as they rapped on the front windows, startling her. Nan jumped at the sudden noise, her arm knocking the flat box off the counter to land upside down at her feet.

"*Crap!*" Looking down at the mess, she felt like stomping her foot in frustration. Not only did she lose her meal, but now she had to take the time to clean up the mess, another delay before she could meet up with Dan.

Nan pulled into the designated parking area at the fairgrounds outside of town thirty minutes later, waving to Sydney and Tamara who stood in line with their husbands for one of the wilder amusement rides. A sudden wave of dizziness assailed her as she wound through the crowd, making her way to the opposite side of the rides, games and food carts toward the riding rings. She stumbled to a stop, bracing a hand on a picnic table and one on her stomach as a cramp threatened to buckle her knees.

"Hey, miss, you okay?" a young cowhand stopped to ask, the girl at his side looking at her with concern.

"Fine, thanks. Just the sun and crowd on an empty stomach, I think. Go ahead, enjoy your day." Taking a deep breath, Nan waited a minute after the young couple moved on, letting her stomach settle before taking off again. She spotted Dan's tall form next to his steed, Tank, just inside a makeshift corral, Grayson standing next to him with his stallion. The two of them conversed as they kept watch on the other two horses trotting around in a wide loop carrying amateur riders.

Neither man heard her as she walked up trying desperately to ignore another wave of nausea, but their voices reached her clear as a bell from several feet away, much to her dismay. A tight clutch gripped her chest as the sheriff asked the very question she intended to pose to Dan.

"I saw you leave with Nan again last night. Are you two going to stay with your new arrangement now that she's coping better?" Grayson spoke around the toothpick nestled in the corner of his mouth, his look inquiring.

Nan sucked in a breath against another abdominal cramp and dizzying blur, straining to hear Dan's answer over the noise.

Dan stiffened in hesitation before replying, "I'm just helping a friend through a tough time. Let's leave it at that for now."

Disappointment and regret swamped her, adding to the bile threatening to rise to her throat. She stumbled back then spun around to leave before they saw her. Given the state she was in, she wouldn't be able to hide her emotions from either man's astute gaze. Moving as fast as her upset stomach allowed, she made it halfway back to the parking lot before sickness forced her to sink down onto the nearest bench. Tears pricked the back of her eyes, which pissed her off. She'd never wept over a man and didn't intend to start now. But, God, his words hurt, the pain making her realize how much she cared, how deep her longing for more with Dan went.

Alice appeared at her side unexpectedly, wearing a concerned frown. "Here, Nan, let me help you. Goodness, you're white as a sheet." Wrapping an arm around her shoulders, Alice's free hand went to Nan's head, checking for a fever.

"You're not warm. In fact, you feel cool, considering the warm afternoon."

The conciliatory words and tone bounced off Nan's misery and she didn't have the strength or willpower to say no when Alice helped her to her feet and guided her over to her parked car.

"Let me drive you to the clinic, dear, before you collapse. Why, you're shaking like a leaf," she crooned, opening the passenger door on a small coupe.

Something wasn't registering right, but Nan couldn't pinpoint what it was through the pounding of her head, the nausea threatening to come up and the pain encompassing her heart. Not until she roused enough to notice Alice was driving away from Willow Springs at a fast clip.

"Alice…" She struggled to sit up against the tight confines of the seatbelt.

"Shut up, bitch," the older woman snarled in a hateful voice Nan didn't recognize. "I need to think. If only you would have cooperated with my plans, I could be on my way home by now."

Confusion and a kernel of fear added to Nan's misery. "What are you talking about…" And then, like a flick of a light switch, enlightenment dawned and she squinted her blurry eyes. "*You?* You're behind all the strange things happening to me, aren't you?"

"Give the girl a prize," Alice sneered, pressing harder on the accelerator. "I hoped I put enough Visine in the brownies to at least put you in a coma. That would have been enough to delay Gerard's trial until I could finish the job or get someone to finish it for me."

Nan was trying to assimilate what Alice was saying, but only two words registered, both confusing her more. "Visine? Gerard? Who *are* you?"

Shaking her head, Alice gripped the steering wheel and the cold eyes she leveled on Nan answered one question. "Shit, you're Gerard's mother." And as much of a whack-a-doodle as her son, it appeared. Why hadn't she caught the resemblance before? There was no mistaking who her son had inherited his cold black eyes from.

"Damn right, and no one hurts my boy, especially not some two-bit floozy." She chuckled, the sound of pure evil raising the hairs on Nan's arms. "Research was so easy. Visine. Who would ever think such a product could be so dangerous if ingested? It's the tetrahydrozoline that can render someone incapacitated, make them so sick." She frowned and her mouth twisted into an ugly sneer. "Why didn't you eat the brownies? I made sure to add a large enough dose to put you in the hospital."

"I did." And then Nan remembered getting violently ill, throwing everything up just minutes upon waking, right after Dan had arrived. At the time she'd thought it odd since she'd been holding her alcohol since college. The combination of bourbon and the tainted brownies must have been enough to purge herself of the possible poisonous effects. A slow rage started to unfurl deep inside her as the puzzling incidents of the past weeks came rushing back. "You picked up my purse, copied my key and put it back. Did you poison my yogurt and the biscuits and gravy?" The image of the poor tom cat popped into her head, but at least something good had come from spilling the diner order earlier. One bite shouldn't have any detrimental or lasting effects.

"And yet here you still are." Alice wanted to cackle with glee. The shock and anger turning Nan's face red was priceless. Now, if she could just figure out where to dump her body, she could get back to her precious son who didn't deserve to go to jail because of this bitch. "I have to tell you, that scene in the library was priceless. It couldn't have gone better if I had planned that one. Instead, you fell right into the role of a muddled head case. It took you long enough to change your lock. Everyone in this town is way too trusting. Idiots," she scoffed.

"Willa certainly is. How did you manage that?"

She chuckled. "That was easy. I kept tabs on you in New Orleans and knew as soon as you boarded a plane for home. Thanks to you telling my son all about your hometown and your love of reading, I knew where you were going and had some way to ingratiate myself into your life. I learned about the librarian's luncheon in Billings before leaving Louisiana and winged it arranging to meet the Willow Springs librarian. Where does that road go?" She pointed to the right at the upcoming intersection.

Nan wasn't about to help her. In fact, she didn't plan on riding along with the raving lunatic much farther. Enough of this bullshit. She was done with the Avets controlling her life and she saw her opportunity as Alice slowed to take the turn.

"Nowhere I'm going with you, you deranged psychopath." Pressing the release on the seatbelt, she lunged across the seat, reaching for the steering wheel to yank the car into the field. She hadn't counted on the gun, or the blow to her temple that stunned her into seeing stars as she fell back against the seat.

Pete knew he was making a mistake yet found himself helpless to turn around and return to the ranch. He owed Dan a debt of gratitude for giving him a second chance once he was released from prison and the army, one he would have had trouble repaying before he let the nightmares get the best of him this morning. If he didn't find the strength to veer from this course, he would never get the chance to not only repay his boss but start a future as his permanent employee. Guilt gnawed at his gut as he drove toward Billings, and the connection to drugs he had made. He couldn't fight it anymore, couldn't get through the day without the peaceful oblivion the drugs offered from the screams of the dying he'd been powerless to help.

I'm a failure, and that will never change. He blinked, fighting the gathering dampness blurring his vision as he thought he recognized Ms. Meyers as the passenger in the vehicle up ahead. Hadn't Dan mentioned before leaving this morning he would be meeting up with her at the fair? Pete, Morales and Bertie had gotten a kick out of ribbing their boss over his interest in the woman, surprised when he didn't deny he'd planned on it being permanent. Curiosity, and a nagging sense of worry prodded him into sending a quick text to Dan, adding he thought something might be wrong when the car swerved from the erratic driving of whoever was behind the wheel.

Ten minutes later, Pete was wrestling over whether to continue going straight past the upcoming intersection and on into Billings in pursuit of temporary numbness from his pain, or to stay with Ms. Meyers until he was sure she would be okay. *She looks fine and is not my problem. I need...* "Son-of-a-bitch!" he swore aloud as the driver brought down the butt of a gun on her temple when Ms. Meyers lunged toward her, making a grab for the wheel.

Making a lightning fast decision, praying it wasn't a mistake and landed her in more danger, he swung right, cutting off the car as it slowed to make the turn, hoping his impact on the rear end didn't cause her more harm.

Dan checked the time again, wondering what the hell was keeping Nan. When Grayson asked him about their relationship, he'd wanted nothing more than to admit to his feelings and hope they could make their current arrangement permanent. But Nan deserved to hear that first and he was itching to clear the air between them as soon as possible. As late morning passed into early afternoon with no sign of her, his eagerness turned to annoyance. Regardless of their previous relationship, or the reason for their bargain that was supposed to only last until she had overcome her trauma, he was tired of her pulling away from him. When he got his hands on her again, he planned to lay it on the line, tell her in no uncertain terms how they would be going forward and reinforcing his intentions with a long, overdue spanking.

As Grayson returned leading his horse carrying the last rider for now, Dan pulled out his phone to call Nan, tired of waiting. Seeing a missed text, he started to pull it up when another one came in, this one making his blood run cold as fear threatened all rational sense.

"What's wrong?" Grayson's sharp, demanding tone broke through Dan's paralyzing disbelief as he thrust Pete's message toward him. He scanned the message then said exactly what Dan was thinking. "Fuck, let's go."

"Take over," Dan called out to the college kid helping at the riding ring. Without waiting for a reply, he jumped into the passenger seat of Grayson's cruiser parked in the field outside the makeshift coral.

"We'll head north, cut across the bluff and reach that corner in five minutes. What the hell's going on?" Grayson floored the accelerator, bouncing the SUV over the rough terrain with a tight grip on the wheel and a concerned frown darkening his face.

"I don't know, just step on it," Dan growled as he read the previous text, thankful Pete had noticed Nan and followed when the driver's behavior looked suspicious. He couldn't come up with a plausible reason for her to be on that road instead of at the fair with him, but given the harassment of the past few weeks, he wasn't leaving anything to chance.

They cleared the rise above the backroads intersection just in time to watch Pete ram his truck into the back of a compact sedan. Grayson sped forward, both of them swearing and reaching for the rifle on the rack above the seat as Nan stumbled from the car as soon as it stalled. Dan saw red when he noticed the trickle of blood dripping down from her forehead and vowed someone would pay for hurting her.

Disoriented, Nan fell to the grassy ground then struggled to her feet, fearing for her life. Her heart pounded with the panic clamping her throat closed as two shots rent the air, one slamming into Pete's shoulder as he rushed forward and tackled her back to the ground with a heavy grunt, the other sending Alice flying backward with a neat hole in her forehead.

"No!" Scooting out from under her protector's body, she scrambled to her knees, frantically pressing her hands against Pete's blood-soaked shoulder, tears streaming down her face. "Where did you come from? Who…" She sobbed, saying, "You saved my life."

Pete offered a weak smile, reaching up to grip her hand, his pale face reflecting calm relief. "No, ma'am. Believe it or not, I think you saved mine."

And then Grayson and Dan were there, taking over as the sheriff checked to ensure Alice was dead and Dan stooped down next to them, pulling a roll of gauze from a medical kit.

"It looks like it went right through." Wrapping the bandaging around the wound to stem the flow of blood, he looked into Pete's painfilled eyes and whispered, "Thank you."

Nan kept hold of his hand, the chain of events a jumbled blur as she replayed Pete's timely interference followed by Dan and Grayson's arrival. All she knew for certain was life was too short to second guess feelings. With sirens and flashing lights heralding the arrival of more cops and an ambulance, abundant questions that needed answering and her body racked with nausea and pain, she turned on Dan as Grayson helped Pete stand. Heedless of who heard, she grabbed his shirt, pulling up onto her toes with a furious whisper. "Damn it, Shylock, what we used to have, that was before…"

She choked as he lowered his head, his dark eyes as warm as the brush of his lips over hers and his voice. "That was then, and this is now. I love you, Nan." A euphoric sense of relief flooded her system as she sagged against him, convinced the trauma of her past was finally over.

Dan's words and his hovering, protective presence the next few hours eased the stress of getting her stomach pumped and going over the series of events with Grayson that had resulted in Alice's death and Pete's injury. There were no words for Nan to express her deep gratitude to Dan's troubled employee, or how much more she now resented the Avet family for what Gerard and his mother had put her through. As Dan drove her home from Billings several hours later, she nodded off against his shoulder, relaxing and feeling good for the first time all day.

Dan stripped Nan and settled her in his bed before undressing and joining her. God, he was tired, he admitted, pulling her into his arms, relishing her soft curves molding to his side. He didn't know how long it would take to dislodge his heart from his throat, where it had been stuck since seeing that crazed woman aiming a gun at Nan. Nothing could have clarified his feelings so effectively or cemented his future intentions faster than coming close to losing her yet again. He owed Pete a debt he could never repay and hoped he took him up on his offer to stay on at the ranch after his probation was up. From the way he'd left Bertie hovering over Pete in the barracks, he knew his foreman would ensure Pete's acceptance.

He still wasn't happy Grayson had taken the shot Dan felt should have been his. His friend's terse reply, "I'm the sheriff, less paperwork," did little to appease him after Nan relayed the scope of Alice Avet's attempts to delay and discredit her testimony against Gerard while sitting in the emergency room being pumped full of toxin-killing drugs. Tightening his arms around her, he settled on gratitude for good timing and pure blind luck.

"So," Nan whispered against his chest, her soft breath stirring his nipple into puckering, "how long do you think we've felt this way about each other?"

A low rumble of laughter shook his chest. "Longer than either of us will admit. I'm sure there's a lesson to be learned there."

Nan giggled, a rare sound coming from her as she pulled away and climbed on top of him. Straddling his hips, she reached down to grip his straining cock. "The only lessons I'm interested in learning are those that can make me feel this," she lowered herself by slow increments onto his shaft, "good." She sighed as she settled her soft, plump ass on his groin.

With her snug pussy hugging his rock-hard flesh, he gripped her hips and lifted, dragging his rigid length along her slick walls. "Then I'll get started teaching right away."

Dan's heart finally settled back into his chest as she arched above him, crying out, "I love you, Master Dan," as he surged up inside her.

Epilogue

Two months later

The bailiff opened the door into the front of the courtroom and nodded at Nan. "They're ready for you, miss."

Rising from the hall bench, she ran clammy palms down her sides before crossing the hall on rubbery legs. No matter how many times she told herself she could handle seeing Gerard again, she continued to wonder if that were true. Despite the hours Dan spent tutoring her on her testimony, giving her pointers, telling her what to say, and not say to certain questions, a small sliver of insecurity remained.

Offering her a smile of encouragement, the bailiff ushered her forward with a wave of his hand. "Deep breath, miss. Everything will be fine."

"Let's hope," she replied, gazing into the courtroom. Instead of looking toward the defendant's table, she sought the front row, every roiling emotion inside her settling when she saw the two most important people in her life sitting side by side. With Dan and Jay there, giving her their undivided support, how could she go wrong? Seeing Tamara, Sydney and Avery behind them was icing on the cake, their surprise presence sending a warm glow coursing through her. If they were in New Orleans, Nan didn't doubt their husbands were here also.

Her heart rolled over as she entered, taking the first step toward a bright and promising future.

The End

BJ Wane

I live in the Midwest with my husband and our two dogs, a Poodle/Pyrenees mix and an Irish Water Spaniel. I love dogs, spending time with my daughter, babysitting her two dogs, reading and working puzzles. We have traveled extensively throughout the states, Canada and just once overseas, but I much prefer being a homebody. I worked for a while writing articles for a local magazine but soon found my interest in writing for myself peaking. My first book was strictly spanking erotica, but I slowly evolved to writing erotic romance with an emphasis on spanking. I love hearing from readers and can be reached here: bjwane@cox.net.

Recent accolades include: 5 star, Top Pick review from The Romance Reviews for *Blindsided*, 5 star review from Long & Short Reviews for Hannah & The Dom Next Door, which was also voted Erotic Romance of the Month on LASR, and my most recent title, Her Master At Last, took two spots on top 100 lists in BDSM erotica and Romantic erotica in less than a week!

Visit her Facebook page
https://www.facebook.com/bj.wane
Visit her blog here
bjwane.blogspot.com

Don't miss these exciting titles by BJ Wane and Blushing Books!

Single Titles
Claiming Mia

Cowboy Doms Series
Submitting to the Rancher, Book 1
Submitting to the Sheriff, Book 2
Submitting to the Cowboy, Book 3
Submitting to the Lawyer, Book 4

Virginia Bluebloods Series
Blindsided, Book 1
Bind Me To You, Book 2
Surrender To Me, Book 3
Blackmailed, Book 4
Bound By Two, Book 5
Determined to Master: Complete Series

Murder On Magnolia Island:
The Complete Trilogy
Logan - Book 1
Hunter - Book 2
Ryder - Book 3

Miami Masters
Bound and Saved - Book One
Master Me, Please - Book Two
Mastering Her Fear - Book Three
Bound to Submit - Book Four
His to Master and Own - Book Five
Theirs to Master - Book Six

Masters of the Castle
Witness Protection Program
(Controlling Carlie)

Connect with BJ Wane
bjwane.blogspot.com

Printed in February 2023
by Rotomail Italia S.p.A., Vignate (MI) - Italy